Also by J.A. Lang

Chef Maurice and a Spot of Truffle (Book 1)
Chef Maurice and the Wrath of Grapes (Book 2)

Paperback edition published by Purple Panda Press

Copyright © J.A. Lang 2015

J.A. Lang has asserted her right under the Copyright, Designs and Patents Act 1988 to be identified as the author of this work.

ISBN 978 1 910679 08 1

CHEF MAURICE
AND THE
BUNNY-BOILER BAKE OFF

J.A. Lang

PURPLE
PANDA
PRESS

To T.

CHAPTER 1

The dead body lay stretched out across the table, next to a tub of coarse sea salt and cracked black pepper and a large bowl of freshly chopped sage and thyme.

Chef Maurice, proprietor and head chef of Le Cochon Rouge, the only restaurant in the little village of Beakley, stood with his arms folded, staring down critically at the kitchen's newest visitor.

"He is not very big. You told them, *non*, that we required the largest of their *cochons* for tomorrow?" He shot a questioning glance at Patrick, his sous-chef.

"*Oui*, chef. They promised me that this is their largest. And come on, look at it. We're barely going to be able to get it into the spit roaster. Plus we'll need to adjust the overnight cooking times for the extra weight. I did some calculations. I reckon we'll need to start the roast at least an hour and a half earlier now."

They stood in silence, contemplating the fine-looking specimen laid out before them: eighty kilos of Gloucestershire Old Spot, purchased from a rare breed pig farmer over near Cirencester.

"*Bof*, he will do," said Chef Maurice grudgingly. He grabbed a fistful of salt and pepper and got to work rubbing the seasoning all over one meaty shoulder. "Alf, the apples. They are ready for the making of the sauce?"

Alf, Le Cochon Rouge's commis chef, was a gangly young lad who had embarked upon a culinary career under the mistaken belief that being a chef involved a lot of flaming pans, flashing knives, and, he had hoped, the chance to meet a perky young waitress or two.

Unfortunately, as the lowliest member of the Cochon Rouge kitchen crew, he had thus far only managed to encounter a copious amount of vegetables requiring peeling, endless giant pots of slowly simmering stock, and Dorothy, the restaurant's long-time head waitress, who was roughly the same age as his own mother and had *views* on the perkiness of today's young women. (It was, she claimed, mostly the fault of overzealous engineering on the part of today's lingerie manufacturers.)

"Almost done, chef," he called, from his station over by the walk-in fridge. He was standing beside a jumbo-sized pot filled with chopped apples and surrounded by a snake's nest of peelings.

"Dearie me, he's a big 'un, isn't he?" said Dorothy, appearing through from the dining room, a stack of finished dessert plates in each hand.

In other restaurants, lunch was often treated as a light, fleeting affair, but Chef Maurice had a typical Frenchman's

2

opinion on the correct length and quantity of a proper *déjeuner*, and was quite willing to unleash a slew of complimentary desserts on any new diners who thought they could get away with only a main dish and a glass of water for their midday meal.

(Secretaries in the Oxfordshire area now made sure to book a two-hour post-lunch slot of 'meetings' into their bosses' calendars following any appointment involving 'lunch at C. Rouge, Beakley'—along with the provision of pillows on their desk, a Do Not Disturb sign for the door, and a fizzing glass of Alka-Seltzer, just in case.)

"You should have seen us earlier," said Patrick, as he firmly massaged a handful of sage-and-thyme rub onto the porky haunch before him. "Took all three of us to get it out of the van." He didn't mention that it had been mostly himself and Alf doing the lifting, as Chef Maurice hovered around, continuing to lament the size of his purchase.

"You brought that thing in through the backyard?" said Dorothy, with a disapproving look.

"*Non, non*, do not worry about *le petit* Hamilton," said Chef Maurice. "He did not see us. Of this, I made certain."

Hamilton, the restaurant's resident micro-pig, had been adopted last autumn by Chef Maurice as part of a series of events that had ended in the arrest of a pignapping murderer. Since then, the little pig had settled happily into his home in the scrubby field behind the restaurant, which bordered on Le Cochon Rouge's backyard.

"Are you sure he didn't see you? Sight like that could traumatise the little dear for life." Like the other members of staff, Dorothy had a special place in her heart for the newest curly-tailed addition to the Cochon Rouge family.

"*Oui*, I made sure that he would take his afternoon nap a little early today. He now sleeps like *un bébé*."

"He went and put a shot of cognac in Hamilton's water bowl," said Patrick, shaking his head.

"Well, I suppose it won't do 'im too much harm, long as he doesn't get a taste for the stuff." Dorothy lowered the stacks of dishes into the sink. "Everyone's been askin' me if we're doing the hog roast again this year. I told 'em they best get to the front of the queue when lunchtime starts. You know, they say this year's Fayre's going to be the biggest we've had so far. Reckon it must be 'cause of all those celebrity posters they've been putting up. And of course, the Great Beakley Bake Off always brings 'em in, too."

"Bah! I say again, what need do we have of celebrities at our Fayre?"

"It's only one celebrity, chef," said Patrick.

"Hah! That even *you* should call her a 'celebrity chef'—"

"What? I didn't—"

"—just as they do on the television and the newspapers. A chef is not the same as a cook! And she cannot even do that!" Chef Maurice pounded a fist on the table, causing the bowl of herb rub to dance dangerously close

4

to the edge. "You have seen how she makes her spaghetti carbonara with the double cream?"

Chef Maurice may have been French, but he stood in solid support of his Italian colleagues in the argument that a proper carbonara sauce should be made with eggs and pancetta and parmesan and *nothing else*.

"I thought you didn't watch her show, chef," said Alf, sweeping up the apple peelings into a bowl for Hamilton's dinner.

Chef Maurice harrumphed. "Sometimes, it cannot be helped. When the television is already on . . ."

"Sure, chef," said Patrick with a grin. He was fully aware that, like the little old lady who watches the all-day music channels in order to complain in righteous horror about the state of today's youth and their gyrating buttocks (the youths', that was), Chef Maurice had never been known to miss an episode of Miranda Matthews' cookery show, not since she had made her screen debut over twenty years ago in the dubiously named sensation: *Cook It Right!*

Nowadays, her cookbooks sold in their millions every Christmas, and reruns of her various series were a staple of weekday evening television. An enthusiastic traveller, Miranda Matthews had tried her hand at nearly every major world cuisine, though rumours were that the Japanese government had ordered her deportation after her attempt to film a show on their shores involving recipes such as pan-fried sushi and green-tea-flavoured sausages. The older male population of Britain also harboured rather fond memories of one of her

5

earlier shows, entitled *Beach Bites*, in which she'd conducted the entirety of the filming wearing only a bikini and high heels and slicked in so much suntan oil that standing next to an open flame constituted a serious fire hazard.

"—and for the committee to allow such a woman onto the Bake Off judging panel, it is surely a crime of the highest nature!" continued Chef Maurice.

His staff offered their various conciliatory mutterings. They all knew very well that their head chef's main bone of contention was not that Miranda Matthews had been given a seat on the Bake Off judging panel, but that she had been given *his* seat.

One that his somewhat expansive buttocks had been warming for several years previously.

"But," he said finally, "I have now devised a plan to regain my position."

"A legal one?" said Patrick, suspiciously.

Chef Maurice ignored his sous-chef. "At tonight's committee meeting, I will present a most urgent reason why I should return to the panel. Alf, you have completed the preparations?"

"*Oui*, chef," said Alf, pulling out a thick folder of photocopied newspaper clippings.

"*Bien*, I will take it with me tonight. Now, Alf, continue here with the rubbing of the spices. I must start the making of the special mustard."

Le Cochon Rouge's secret mustard sauce was famous throughout the county as an accompaniment to a good slab

6

of chargrilled steak, used in the glaze for the restaurant's honey-and-mustard roast chicken, and, of course, slathered thickly onto a warm hog roast roll. No one except Chef Maurice knew the recipe, but there was speculation that the ingredients included two bottles of the finest amontillado sherry, a type of molasses only available in two American states, and, according to some sources, a variety of bay leaf only grown on the windier slopes of the Greek island of Meganisi.

When questioned, Chef Maurice would only stroke his large moustache and admit that, *oui*, the speaker might be correct. But then again, they might not.

"I do hope chef's not plannin' anything *too* drastic," said Dorothy, as she watched Patrick and Alf continue on with the hog roast preparations.

"You never know, when it comes to chef," said Patrick darkly.

However, it would turn out that someone else had also been making plans regarding certain members of the Bake Off judging panel. But unlike those of Chef Maurice, their plans would turn out to have some rather more deadly consequences.

CHAPTER 2

Like many organisations of dubious national significance, the Beakley Spring Fayre Committee applied itself to its duties with a seriousness directly proportional to the committee's view of its own importance.

That is to say, they took things very seriously indeed.

This was particularly true in the case of Miss Edith Caruthers—the Spring Fayre Committee Chair, as well as the long-standing doyenne of the Beakley Ladies' Institute—who regarded their purpose as nothing less than internationally vital to the success of county and country. Visitors came from miles around to attend the Beakley Spring Fayre, a highlight of the Cotswolds social calendar, and it was imperative that everything tomorrow run as smoothly as butter across a hot pan.

Parking arrangements had been discussed and debated, the capacity of the temporary toilet facilities had been double-checked against visitor number projections, and a subtle yet significant last-minute alteration to the layout of the stands had been made such that the blown-glass and fine china stall was no longer next to the archery butts.

Finally, with the schedule for the cookery demonstration tent now honed to military precision, there was only one more problem left to tackle.

"Mr Manchot," said Miss Caruthers, glaring over her glasses at Chef Maurice, "for the last time, I can assure you that every single risk and danger to our Bake Off judges has been thoroughly considered and mitigated as part of our Health and Safety assessment. It will therefore be perfectly safe and healthy for *all* of them to take part in the judging of the cake contest."

"Ah, you may think this is so, but I have the evidence to prove that this is incorrect," said Chef Maurice. He pulled out the stack of newspaper clippings that Alf had collected for him.

"One may think there is no danger, but when you look carefully, *voilà*, the truth appears. In Scotland, there were three judges made most ill at this year's Annual Haggis Championship, and last year, there was found an explosive hidden in a giant scone at the Devon Clotted Cream Festival! And we must not forget the incident not far from here involving a most fatal quiche . . ."

He threw the pile of Fayre-related fatalities onto the table. "It is clear. Tomorrow, Madame Caruthers, the Bake Off judges face a grave danger!"

Miss Caruthers gave him a severe look—though whether this was due to the topic of conversation, or her having been upgraded to 'madame' due to her advanced age in the French chef's eyes, one could not be certain.

"And I suppose, Mr Manchot, that your solution to this imminent peril is that you should be allowed back onto the judging panel?"

"*Exactement!*" Chef Maurice beamed, pleased that the Committee Chair was, for once, showing some good sense.

"Rather daring of you, don't you think, in the face of all this evidence?"

"Ah, but *non, madame.* For the nose of a chef, it is most delicate, like that of a foxhound." He tapped his own, large, example. "I will place myself as the first to taste each baking entry, and so will be ready to make an alert in the case of any danger. It is, you see, a matter of duty!"

The rest of the committee turned, as one, back to Miss Caruthers, who deployed a thin smile in Chef Maurice's direction.

"Very gallant of you, Mr Manchot. But even so, I'm afraid I will have to ask the judges to take their chances. As we've discussed previously, there is simply no space on the judging table for another taster this year."

"Then one must be replaced!"

There was an intake of breath around the table.

"Impossible," said Miss Caruthers calmly. "I'm sure you'll agree that, as Chair of this committee, as well as Head Judge of the Beakley Ladies' Annual Cake Challenge, I am obligated to sit on the panel. And of course, there's no question of replacing Mayor Gifford, who's kindly agreed to come over from Cowton to open the Fayre—"

And who was, incidentally, the husband of Mrs Angie

Gifford, the mousy-haired Secretary of the Beakley Ladies' Institute. Angie was currently engaged in nibbling on a Rich Tea biscuit and watching the proceedings with a certain amount of alarm.

"—and I assume you can't object to Chef Elizabeth's inclusion, a lady whose, ahem, nose you cannot possibly disparage—"

Chef Maurice frowned. Chef Elizabeth was one of Britain's top pastry chefs—though, in his opinion, pastry chefs as a bunch were generally far more concerned with the look of their creations than the aroma. Still, the woman was travelling down from her restaurant specially for the Fayre, and plus, he had other reasons for not wanting to unduly displease Chef Elizabeth.

"—nor can you possibly expect to ask that Miranda Matthews step down—"

"An insult to our profession," muttered Chef Maurice, but even he knew it would be a futile task to try and bump a celebrity chef off the judging panel, especially as it was her face that had been put on all the Bake Off posters and plastered up and down the Cotswolds.

"—and lastly, there's Mr Wordington-Smythe—"

"Who will face any ill-mannered icing and perilous pastry with a brave countenance and an iron constitution," said Arthur Wordington-Smythe, Chef Maurice's best friend and esteemed food critic for the *England Observer*.

The latter was a role that had lately been taking somewhat of a toll on his usually trim waistline, causing his wife Meryl

11

to institute a new dietary regime within the Wordington-Smythe household. Under such circumstances, Arthur was not about to give up a chance to spend an afternoon partaking in the unfettered consumption of home-baked desserts and pastries—all in the name of the civic good, of course.

"Nice try though, old chap," said Arthur, as they filed out of the village hall into the cool, still air of a Beakley springtime evening.

"Humph. Madame Caruthers, she will regret to have ignored my warnings."

"I still don't see why you're so desperate to get back onto the tasting panel. You complained all the way through last year's competition, may I remind you."

"That is not the point, *mon ami*. It is the principle! Madame Caruthers dares to suggest I do not have the tasting skills to be a judge."

"I don't think," said Arthur carefully, "that it was your taste buds *per se* that were being called into question."

"Then what?"

"Let's just say that the committee didn't agree on the acceptability of telling a five-year-old that her jam roly-poly 'tastes and looks like a badger sat on it'."

"But I only intended—"

"And then you went on to describe Mr Evans' red velvet cake as 'a tragedy with the flavour of crayons and the look of blood-soaked murder'."

"It is not proper, for a cake to be so *red*." Chef Maurice gave a little shudder. "So they do not enjoy my opinions?

Perhaps that is true. But it is still"—he waved the newspaper clippings—"a grand mistake to leave me from the judging panel. You will see."

Arthur rolled his eyes heavenwards as they continued their stroll up past the village green. "Maurice, I assure you, no one is going to die during the Great Beakley Bake Off."

Le Cochon Rouge sat at the top of Beakley, occupying an old stone cottage which had started life as the village pub, and still bore the original thick oak beams, low stone-arched doorway (treacherous to the occasional over-inebriated diner) and uneven flagstones (ditto) worn smooth by centuries of hungry travellers and thirsty Beakley locals.

PC Lucy, currently off duty from her role as Beakley's only resident police officer, sat in the dining room by the unlit fireplace, sipping on a glass of chilled white wine and mopping up the last of her *moules marinière* with a chunk of crusty bread. She surveyed the empty mussel shells piled high in the upturned dish lid and mused, not for the first time, on the advantages of having a fully trained chef as one's boyfriend.

Patrick, the chef and boyfriend in question, sat opposite her, head bent over a stack of paperwork. "Sorry about this," he'd said when she'd arrived after her shift. "It's just that it's the month end, and you know what chef is like . . ."

PC Lucy had nodded understandingly. Chef Maurice's previous attempts to navigate the world of accountancy had produced roughly the same results as a bunch of monkeys let loose with a calculator and a ballpoint pen. Thankfully for all concerned, nowadays he was more than happy to leave the details to his trusty sous-chef, while enquiring periodically into the health of the annual cheese budget.

"Is Maurice doing his usual demo at the Fayre tomorrow?" she said, as Patrick set aside another stack of invoices.

"Nope, I'm doing it this year. I'll be demonstrating how to fillet and pan-fry a lemon sole."

"What, no flambéing?" Chef Maurice's annual set piece was a guaranteed crowd-pleaser, especially amongst the younger pyromaniacs in the audience.

"The fire department made a specific request to the committee. Chef threw a fit, obviously. Now he's dead set on trying to flambé the hog roast at lunchtime. I've been hiding all the Calvados, just in case." Patrick threw a guilty glance towards the old travel trunk by the door. "Are you going to the Fayre tomorrow?"

"In my official capacity, yes."

In fact, the majority of the Cowton and Beakley Constabulary had all apparently decided that this year's Spring Fayre warranted an increased level of police presence, a decision no doubt unrelated to the unseasonably fine spring weather that Oxfordshire was currently experiencing.

"Are you entering the Bake Off?" asked Patrick, flicking through a thick ring binder of wine invoices.

"You're joking, right? After the last fiasco?"

Last month, under Patrick's patient instruction, PC Lucy had undertaken the creation of a triple-layered chocolate fudge cake for PC Sara's birthday. Each layer had come out of the oven as flat and solid as a manhole cover, and the chocolate icing, once dried, had required the application of a small hacksaw when it came to the cake-cutting.

"It did look fantastic, though," said Patrick. He threw a glance at the clock above the fireplace, and pulled another stack of invoices towards him.

"Are you expecting more tables?" said PC Lucy, looking around the dining room. There were a couple of locals hanging around the bar, tended to by Dorothy. Other than them, though, the evening service seemed to have wound down a long time ago.

Patrick looked up from a rare-breed beef invoice. "Sorry? Oh, no. We're done for the night. I just wanted to get this all done before my mother arrives."

He filed the invoice neatly under 'Expenditure, Meat, Bovine' and was about to start on the next when he noticed a certain quality in the silence emanating from the other side of the table. It was the type of silence that boyfriends and husbands sooner or later learnt to recognise.

"Your mother's coming to visit? And you didn't think to give me any warning?"

Patrick looked puzzled. "It's not like she's a hurricane. You'll like her, I promise."

"Still, it would have been nice to have known a little earlier. I'd have changed out of uniform, at least." PC Lucy looked down ruefully at her slightly scuffed black boots— great for navigating the village's cobbled streets, but perhaps less suitable for making a good first impression—and tried ineffectually to smooth down the slight frizz that often developed in her fine blond hair at the end of a long day.

"She knows I'm a police officer, right?"

"Well, um . . ."

It was an 'um' with harmonics. The same type of 'um' often employed by the male of the species when questioned about anniversary dates, whether the washing had been taken in before the recent downpour, and the exact thought process that could possibly lead one to return from the shops without the milk but carrying a jumbo-pack of iced buns that 'happened to be on offer'.

"You *have* at least told her about me, haven't you?"

"Um . . ."

"Patrick!"

"It's not like I meant *not* to tell her. It's just that, well, it never came up."

"What do you mean, it never—"

She stopped as the restaurant's front door swung open, and a tall woman in her early sixties entered, wheeling a small black suitcase. She had the same dark curly hair as Patrick, though hers was now streaked with grey and cut in a bob, and the same serious brows and sharp brown eyes.

"Hi, darling." She embraced her son with the brief perfunctoriness common to many an English family reunion. Her eyes, though, showed genuine warmth as she ran her gaze over her son's face.

"Hi, Mum. Was the train down okay?"

"The usual. We were delayed at Reading for three-quarters of an hour for no apparent reason, and you can't get a good cup of coffee on the train for love nor money. So," she said, catching sight of PC Lucy, "are you going to introduce me?"

"Oh. Er, Mum, this is Lucy. Lucy, this is my mum. Beth."

"Ah, so you must be the girlfriend that Patrick keeps completely failing to mention."

PC Lucy stood up, unsure if protocol dictated an awkward but well-intentioned hug or a firm handshake. "How did you—"

"It's a special sixth sense you develop as a mother of an unmarried man in his thirties," said Mrs Merland. "Also, Patrick told me he'd been for a walk the other day to one of those National Trust sites. In my experience, a man under fifty does not go for walks in landscape gardens of his own accord."

PC Lucy saw Patrick shoot her a tentative 'see, it's all okay' smile, and she raised him back a 'we'll see about that' eyebrow.

"So, Mrs Merland—"

"Please, call me Beth."

"Of course. Are you going to be around for the Beakley Spring Fayre tomorrow?"

"I most certainly am," said Mrs Merland, unwinding the lavender scarf from around her neck. "I've heard such lovely things about it. I've not been to a proper country fair in years. Will you be entering the Bake Off?"

Out of the corner of her eye, PC Lucy saw Patrick's look of sudden alarm. As Mrs Merland bent down to fetch a tissue from her handbag, he gave Lucy a vigorous head shake.

The cheek! He didn't think her cakes were good enough for his mother? All right, so Sergeant Burns had mentioned something about a broken crown and a trip to the dentist after her last baking attempt, but she was surely improving. And no one could deny her cakes *looked* pretty good.

"Oh, definitely," replied PC Lucy, with a bright smile. "I love baking. It's so relaxing and so satisfying to create something, you know what I mean?"

"Well, I'll be looking forward to trying a bit of your cake tomorrow, then," said Mrs Merland.

"Actually, I think only the judges get to try the cakes, I'm afraid," said PC Lucy, attempting a look of deep regret.

In truth, she was now feeling a sudden stab of guilt at the idea of subjecting tomorrow's judges to such a jaw-aching ordeal. But, on the plus side, without Chef Maurice on the tasting panel, hopefully the judges would find something positive enough to say to avoid completely embarrassing her in front of Mrs Merland.

There was the sound of raised voices outside and the front door burst open once more, this time to allow the entry of Chef Maurice and Arthur, apparently bickering about the amount of stewed prunes in a steamed pudding necessary to produce a poisonous, or at least highly laxative, effect.

"*Mais non*, one would need at the least— Ah! It is *la bonne* Maman Merland!" cried Chef Maurice, rushing over to deal a properly Gallic slew of kisses to Mrs Merland's cheeks. "And you have been introduced to Mademoiselle Lucy, the most excellent police lady in Oxfordshire?"

"And a keen baker, I hear." Mrs Merland smiled at PC Lucy, while Patrick descended into a sudden fit of coughs.

"Ah?" Chef Maurice's expression, even from behind that giant moustache of his, betrayed that he too had heard about the hacksaw incident.

"I was just saying, Maurice," said Mrs Merland, "I'll have to do my best to be impartial, then, tomorrow on the judging table."

"You're . . . one of the Bake Off judges?" PC Lucy felt her voice leap a few octaves. She didn't dare look at Patrick.

"But of course!" said Chef Maurice, waving them to sit down, while he ambled off behind the bar to fetch his decanter of best cognac. "Madame Elizabeth is one of the finest pastry chefs in all of England! Come, let us celebrate our guest."

"Your mother is an award-winning *pastry chef*?!" hissed PC Lucy to Patrick, as Chef Maurice poured them each a generous measure of amber liquor.

"I did try to warn you—"

"Not good enough!" PC Lucy rubbed her temples. Tomorrow was going to be an unmitigated disaster. She supposed it would be too much to hope, really, that something would happen to get the Bake Off cancelled.

But, still, you never knew . . .

CHAPTER 3

The next morning brought another day of fine English weather. The mild sun and light breeze dried the last of the dewdrops clinging to the grass, and lines of colourful bunting took to the skies as the Beakley Spring Fayre Committee rushed about the field, putting the finishing touches on the decorations.

Due to the Fayre's growing repute—last year they'd even had a busload of visitors from South Korea, which had been viewed as something of an international coup, even if the driver had later confessed he'd taken the wrong turning for Stonehenge—the location for this year's event had been moved from its usual spot on the village green to a large field on the southern edge of Beakley proper. Used occasionally by the local cricket club, it was surrounded by old woodland on both sides, and hemmed in by the main road to the north and by Warren's Creek, a popular paddling stream and punting ground, to the south.

Arthur, who had been tasked with checking that all the stands were properly located on their designated spots, wandered amiably about the wooden stalls and long trestle tables that had sprouted up in the last few hours.

Between the hook-a-duck stand and a purveyor of alarmingly pink candyfloss, he came across Alf standing behind a rickety-looking table. The young commis chef was fiddling with a big old-fashioned weighing scale, on which sat a soup tureen containing a small pig wearing a straw hat.

Above the table was the hand-painted sign: *Guess The Weight Of The Micro Pig!*

Hamilton, the pig in question, was staring around at the stalls nearby. This was his first year attending the Beakley Spring Fayre, and he appeared satisfied to find himself sitting in such a prime spot.

Arthur leaned over to sneak a glance at the needle on the scales. Even after deducting the weight of the average porcelain soup tureen, he was still more than a little surprised.

"My, he's grown quite a bit since the winter, hasn't he? Wonder what Maurice has been feeding him."

Back in the autumn, when Hamilton had first turned up, he could have easily fit into a ladies' shoebox; now, you'd have to at least order a pair of size 12 wellington boots to get him in.

"'Fraid I can't let you enter now," said Alf, stowing the weighing scale away under the table.

"Not a problem, I'm saving my pennies for the coconut shy. Knocked all four of them down last year in one turn—

so much for all those people who say they glue the coconuts on. Did you know I used to bowl for my college cricket team?"

Limbering up his right shoulder in preparation for his signature top-spinner delivery, Arthur strolled off towards the Bake Off tent. Keen amateur bakers had already begun dropping off their icing-covered creations, and one table along the side of the tent was now colonised by a range of ambitious endeavours. There was a hedgehog cake covered in shards of white and milk chocolate, a four-tiered square *genoise* covered in bright yellow royal icing—reminiscent, in Arthur's mind, of a giant Lego pyramid—several versions of the usual carrot cakes and Victoria sponges, and even a few attempts at the classic pink-and-yellow-squared, marzipan-wrapped Battenberg.

At the end of the table, PC Lucy was unboxing a large round cake covered in shiny dark chocolate ganache and decorated with white chocolate curls.

"Need a hand with that?" asked Arthur. "Ganache is always a fuss to transport, isn't it? Always ends up touching the side of the box and getting smudged."

"Not this one," said PC Lucy morosely, sliding the cake onto a glass stand with surprising ease. "Watch this." Before Arthur could stop her, she'd drawn her truncheon and dealt the offending cake a sharp rap to the surface. There was a dull *thunk*.

"I'm thinking of writing to the company that makes those bulletproof vests, to see if they want my recipe."

"Ah, I see." Arthur sought around for a suitably gentlemanly comment. "Well, I'm sure it will taste wonderful. And I don't believe that 'cuttability' is one of the judging criteria, if that helps."

"I tried elbowing it off the kitchen table earlier, when Patrick wasn't looking," said PC Lucy, a haunted look in her eyes. "It *bounced*."

Arthur decided to leave the police officer to her cake-based woes and made his way over to the cookery demonstration tent next door.

Rows of white garden chairs had been laid out across the grassy floor and, up at the front, a small kitchen stage had been constructed, complete with two hobs, a portable oven, and a sink at the back.

A stick-thin woman in her early forties, with an orangeade tan, pink stilettos and caramel hair piled high in an elaborate beehive, was stalking back and forth on the stage, issuing commands to a pair of harried-looking young women who were putting the equipment through its paces.

"Eugh, *gas*," said the stiletto-ed woman, waving a red-taloned hand at the hobs. "I *hate* cooking on gas."

"Most likely because it causes her hairspray to set on fire," said a voice from Arthur's right.

It came from Chef Bonvivant, the pencil-moustached, effortlessly urbane owner of L'Epicure, a fine dining establishment not far from Beakley. He was standing at the back of the tent, arms neatly folded as he watched Miranda Matthews' prima-donna performance. Beside him, Chef

Maurice, also dressed in chef's whites—though his buttons bore significantly more strain around the stomach area than those of Chef Bonvivant—nodded his assent.

"*Oui*. And regard her fingers! She must serve her guests a dinner full of nail lacquer, if she cooks with hands like that." Chef Maurice let out a loud cluck of disapproval.

Arthur was surprised. Usually the pair of Frenchmen got along like two cats in a very small sack, but today they seemed to have set aside their differences to partake in the mutual condemnation of Miranda Matthews.

"You have seen her show on the television?"

"I have watched one episode," said Chef Bonvivant, in the tones of one owning up to a minor predilection of a somewhat risqué nature. "She made oatmeal biscuits from a box of cereal, and burnt them. My nephew, he is four and he cooks better than this woman."

Up on the stage, Miranda Matthews was dealing with an issue of culinary logistics.

"And where are we meant to put the flipping microwave?"

Arthur saw both chefs wince at the mention of the m-word.

"How did it happen that she was invited here in the first place?" said Chef Bonvivant, as they watched Miranda's assistants weave back and forth carrying the giant microwave between them, as Miranda debated the merits of various positions.

"It must be that Madame Caruthers wished to punish me further," said Chef Maurice. "First, she takes away my judging seat, and now *this*!" He waved two outstretched palms towards the stage.

"I heard that Miranda's pretty chummy with one of the Spring Fayre Committee," said Arthur. "And she apparently lives in Cowton, which makes her practically a local."

Cowton, a good-sized market town in the foot of the Cotswolds boasting a chic high street and a two-screen cinema, was a twenty-minute drive from Beakley and the nearest thing the village had to a seething metropolis.

"Which of the Committee?" asked Chef Maurice. "Surely it cannot be Madame Caruthers."

"No, not her." In fact, it was rather hard to imagine Miss Caruthers as being 'chummy' with anyone. Not that she was an unpleasant woman by any definition, but years of headmistressing at the nearby girls' school had left her with a stern countenance and ramrod deportment that deterred anyone from getting too familiar in her presence. "I heard she's an old friend of Angie Gifford," continued Arthur. "They went to school together or something like that."

Chef Maurice nodded, no doubt filing that information away to exact revenge—or at least smaller portions at the restaurant—on poor Angie Gifford for her part in Miranda's presence today.

There was now a small commotion developing up on stage, as a short, rotund man with wavy black hair attempted to grapple with the monster microwave, which had found a home slap bang in the centre of the main counter.

"*Che cavolo?!* What is this thing filled with? Rocks? It cannot stay here! Where will there be space for my pasta-rolling demonstration? It starts in only ten minutes!"

It was Signor Gallo, proprietor of The Spaghetti Tree, one of Cowton's longest-standing restaurants. This apparent longevity was something that irked Arthur to no end; he could only assume that Signor Gallo's fiery temperament and flamboyant showmanship somehow counteracted the near criminal underseasoning of his pasta and the sogginess of his pizza dishes in the eyes of local diners.

"Don't you dare touch my microwave!" yelled Miranda, while her assistants huddled nearby. "Alice, Becky, go get someone to throw this man out of the tent!"

Signor Gallo's feet scrabbled along the stage as he applied his shoulder to the microwave, while Miranda attempted to bat him away with a rubber spatula.

"The fire extinguisher is just outside," Arthur informed the two watching chefs, then ducked out of the tent. He had no desire to be present should something go up in flames, which seemed fairly likely in the current circumstances.

Visitors were starting to stream into the field from the parking area across the road, and various members of the Beakley Ladies' Institute, identifiable by their fetching green-and-white straw boaters, were circulating through the crowd, raffle ticket books at the ready.

Many of the children had come in fancy dress, lured by the prospect of the prize for Best Costume (also unofficially known as the prize for Parent or Guardian with Best Access to Sewing Machine and Large Amounts of Time and Glue). Various pudgy bumblebees were running around with face-painted tigers; there were fairies in pink trainers, budding Spider-men, and a little boy dressed, for some unknown reason, as a giant hot dog.

One particular costume stood out from the crowd. It was worn by a distinguished-looking middle-aged gentleman, and comprised a full-length pastel-pink bunny suit, complete with furry ears and a white bobble tail. There could only be two reasons for a grown man to be dressed thus: doting fatherhood or local politics.

This was a case of the latter.

"Hallo, Arthur!" The rabbit, spotting him, hotfooted its way across the grass to shake his hand. "Splendid day for it, isn't it just?"

"Indeed it is. How's the campaign going?"

Rory Gifford, Mayor of Cowton, gave an expansive shrug. "My people tell me I'm a shoo-in, which probably means they're resting on their laurels a good deal too much. I told them, there'll be no putting our feet up when we get to Westminster."

"Very true." Arthur glanced down at the mayor's own furry examples.

"Fantastic costume, isn't it?" said Angie, coming up beside her husband. She was a short, plump woman with a vague motherly air, though as far as Arthur knew she and Rory didn't have any children. Perhaps her job as cookery teacher at Miss Caruthers' school, having to deal daily with thirty teenage girls wielding knives and hormonal urges, had a dampening effect on any desire to partake in the joy of parenthood.

"My team reckon I'll get more coverage in the papers in this get-up," said Mayor Gifford, tugging at his costume's collar.

"You will, darling. Remember all that fuss last year when Nancy Draykin ran a marathon dressed up as an egg-and-bacon roll, for the children's breakfast club? She even made the national news."

"Only because she had a string of fried bacon tied around her waist and was chased down Cowton High Street by a dozen dogs and one vegetarian," said Mayor Gifford.

"Even so. Oh, isn't that sweet!" Angie pointed across the field to where a small group of children had been coerced into a circle around the old village maypole. Unfortunately, any attempts at weaving and skipping had by this point deteriorated into running madly around, purple and yellow ribbons trailing, while the instructor stood in the middle of it all, rapidly resembling a particularly fashion-forward Egyptian mummy.

"This will be perfect for next month's newsletter! Rory, have you got your phone on you?"

Mayor Gifford reluctantly relinquished his phone to his wife, who handed him an oversized beige leather handbag in return.

"Ooof, what *do* they put in these things?" said Mayor Gifford, as Angie scuttled off towards the maltreated maypole. "Anyway, all she'll come back with is ten pictures of the grass, two of her thumb, and one blurry shot of the actual maypole," he added with a chuckle.

At this point, they were joined by another bunny, except that instead of the baggy plush suit currently sported by Mayor Gifford, this new arrival was wearing a pink corset-and-leotard combination, pink leggings, and a pair of white peep-toe heels. In deference to the concept of rabbit-ness, she was also wearing satin bunny ears in her shoulder-length auburn hair and a white fluffy tail.

"Arthur, this is my top research assistant, Miss Karole Linton," said Mayor Gifford, apparently quite unfazed by the young woman's costume, which was more than could be said for a number of gentlemen milling around nearby.

"Hallo. Mr Wordington-Smythe, isn't it? I recognise you from your restaurant column. Lovely to meet you in person," said Karole, holding out a neatly manicured hand. She had the cut-glass tones of the type of young lady more accustomed to pencil skirts and cashmere cardigans than bunny-girl outfits. Arthur wondered whose idea *her* costume had been.

"Sorry to drag the mayor away," she continued, "but Rory, I thought you should come and say hello to our new Youth Campaign. I've managed to get a few of the local boys interested in putting together a few events—"

With a brief smile at Arthur, she led Mayor Gifford away into the crowd, their white tails bobbing in tandem. Arthur, watching them depart, couldn't help but speculate as to the exact cause of the sudden turnaround in the area's usually politically apathetic youths, and suspected that Miss Karole Linton's shapely ankles, amongst other numerous assets, might have held some sway in the matter.

His stomach gave a little rumble, reminding him that breakfast had been quite a long while ago. Arthur snuck a glance at his watch. If he moved fast, there'd be time for a session at the cupcake-decorating stand, plus the disposal of all evidence thereof, before Meryl made her promised appearance around lunchtime.

At the 'Glam Up Your Cupcake!' stand, he snagged the last seat at the low bench, his knees creaking as he clambered into place between an underage fireman and a ladybug with a dribbly nose.

It had been some time since Arthur had last been required to make small talk with the single-digit age group. He turned to the ladybug on his right. "So, simply splendid weather we've been having, don't you think?"

Come half past eleven, Chef Maurice, Arthur and Patrick had succeeded in securing the last few seats in the back row of the cookery demo tent, with the latter two sitting on either side of Chef Maurice, ready to intervene in the event of heckling, persistent low-level grumbling, or projectile cheese.

Ten stifling minutes rolled by, and Miranda Matthews had still yet to make an appearance up on stage. The tent was packed with culinary enthusiasts of all ages, many of whom were clutching copies of Miranda's latest oeuvre, *Blend It Right!*, a paean to the art of smoothie making.

Chef Maurice jiggled his steel-capped boots and pulled out a battered wristwatch, an item that Patrick had never seen him actually wear. This was not surprising, though, as a professional kitchen involved far too much vegetable rinsing, splattering oil and hot oven doors for one to consider wearing any form of wrist accessory, not to mention the danger of it falling off into the dishes themselves. Diners did not enjoy fishing flies out of their soup, and they certainly had something to say when they found timepieces underneath their *steak minute*.

"*Voilà*, she is late! How does she dare to call herself a chef? To be a chef, one must have the most fine sense of time. For a customer waiting for his food, a delay of ten minutes is a torture. He begins to stare at the food of other diners, he finds the conversation of his table companions to become *intolérable. Non*, to be late, it is unacceptable."

"You could just leave now, you know," said Arthur. "There's plenty of people who'd take your seat, I'm sure."

"Pffft," was all the reply he got to that particular suggestion.

Another tolerably torturous five minutes later, Miranda Matthews strutted in through the back of the tent and up onto the stage. With a little hop, she seated herself up on the kitchen counter and crossed her legs in a flash of pink stiletto.

"Hello there! First, I want to say a *huge* thank you to everyone for coming all the way here to see me today. I've got some real treats lined up for you this session. I'll be showing you how to make my signature vanilla-and-chocolate lava cake—"

"Pah! She simply takes a packet of cake mix and undercooks it—"

"—and I'll also be demonstrating a recipe for a banana-and-yoghurt smoothie from my new book, *Blend It Right!*, which I'll be signing copies of later this afternoon, after the Bake Off—"

"How does she call that a recipe? When I pour cream into my coffee and mix it with a teaspoon, I do not go away and write a book about it!"

"—and finally, I'll be showing you a brand-new celebration cake recipe I've been developing, using everyone's favourite chocolate sweet!" Miranda stretched out her hands in a big *tada* motion towards a giant glass jar of multicoloured Smarties sitting on the counter.

The crowd whispered excitedly to each other. Patrick looked over to Chef Maurice, but his boss was apparently too dumbstruck to comment on this latest revelation.

"In fact"—Miranda paused, then gave her audience a radiant smile—"I *was* going to start with the lava cake, but I can see you're all really excited to see my latest creation. So let's go ahead and start with the Smarties recipe. After all, isn't that the joy of cooking? You always get to start with a blank slate!"

Patrick saw Miranda's two assistants, who were standing half-hidden behind the tent flap, give each other a look of mutual horror, as they threw aside the cake mix boxes they were holding and scrambled to assemble the necessary trays for this sudden change of schedule.

"Aren't they just beautiful?" said Miranda, scooping a handful of Smarties out of the jar and letting them clatter into a bowl in a rainbow of sugar-covered chocolate. "I got my inspiration for this recipe when I took a short trip to India last month. I happened to be in Delhi during the festival of Holi, which"—she nodded at her third assistant, who was standing by the projector screen at the back of the stage—"you might also have heard of as the Festival of Colours."

The screen lit up, though rather dimly due to the bright spring light outside, with photographs of revellers in front of a white-domed temple, their faces and bodies splashed with a riot of colours, with puffs of vivid-hued powder shooting up above their heads. The slideshow ended with a shot of Miranda, free of paint and wearing a white kaftan, leaning over a flower-clad balcony high above the street, smiling beatifically at the tumultuous scene below her. She held a tall glass of smoothie in one hand, and on the little table beside her stood a shiny-new retro-style blender.

"Right! First things first, we'll need something to put these gorgeous Smarties onto. You can make a basic sponge base—there's a recipe for my favourite sponge in *Bake It Right! (Volume 1 of 16)*—but really, the most important part of any celebration cake is the outside, so I won't tell on you if you're skimped for time and use a shop-bought Victoria sponge instead." She aimed a naughty wink at the audience.

Patrick sneaked a glance over at Chef Maurice, who was furiously patting down his pockets and muttering something about 'a special type of hell' for television chefs.

"Ah, and here we are! Thank you, girls," cooed Miranda, graciously accepting a very handsome Victoria sponge cake, oozing with jam and cream, from one of her assistants. She then proceeded to trowel on a thick layer of chocolate icing, pausing occasionally to lick her fingers with a look of lascivious delight.

She was just proceeding to cover the whole thing in careful rows of colour-coordinated Smarties when Patrick's phone alarm buzzed in his pocket. He nudged Chef Maurice, who was busy buffing a tomato on his sleeve.

"We better go get set up, chef," he whispered.

"Eh? Look at how slowly she works. Me, I would have covered ten cakes in this same time—"

"If we don't move now, chef, we're not going to start serving on time." He looked around the tent. "Look. Bonvivant's already gone to set up his stand."

This last fact appeared to get Chef Maurice's attention.

"*Bof*, very well." He aimed one last glare at Miranda Matthews, who was too busy picking out the blue Smarties from her bowl to notice, and heaved himself out of his chair.

"A sponge cake covered in chocolate sweets? The people, they call this cooking?"

"There's probably another step to the recipe, chef." In fact, just as they'd left the tent, Patrick had cast one last backwards glance at the stage, in time to catch Miranda whipping out a set of plastic goggles and firing up a blowtorch.

He decided, however, it was best not to mention this to Chef Maurice.

The battle line was drawn, and the two opposing sides took up position behind their stations, tongs at the ready.

Like in matters of war, politics, and competitive jam eating, when it came to running the most popular lunchtime stall, there could only be one winner.

Chef Maurice hefted up the stainless steel lid on the big wood-fired oven. Hundreds of pounds of slow-roasting hog stared back up at him. By his side, Patrick was busy slicing open a mound of wholegrain cob rolls, while a huge vat of freshly made applesauce bubbled on the portable stove nearby.

To their left, Chef Bonvivant and his kitchen brigade were firing up their hotplates, ready to begin caramelising scallops, piping out creamy cauliflower purée and finally garnishing the finished dish with a crisp slice of dry-cured Italian ham.

"How do they expect those paper plates to hold up to the purée?" whispered Patrick, as they watched their rivals attempt a sample plate for Chef Bonvivant's inspection.

Chef Maurice shook his head. "There is a time for haute cuisine," he said, waving his third 'just for testing' hog roast roll, "and there is not. A good chef must consider his audience. Once we have finished serving up Arnaud"—he patted the curved oven lid—"there will be no question as to who is the greater chef!"

"I wish you'd stop naming our hog roast each year," said Patrick, brushing a generous daub of slow-cooked onion mayonnaise onto the inside of each roll. "It's starting to freak the kids out."

"Bah, they must learn about their food. Last week, there was a little girl in the restaurant who did not know where eggs came from. Can you believe this?"

"Was that the table who Dorothy said left straight after their starters? And hardly touched their *omelette aux herbes fines*?"

Chef Maurice puffed out his chest. "It is not my fault that the parents of today do not inform their children of the key facts of food production."

"I think it was the hand gestures you made when explaining it all, more than the facts, that did it, according to Dorothy . . ."

"Hi, guys. I thought I'd come get our order in before the lunch rush," said PC Lucy, strolling up to the stand. She was in normal uniform, but had managed to pin a daffodil

37

to her walkie-talkie pouch to show willing. "Three jumbo rolls and two regular ones, all with the special mustard, please."

"How's the competition for the Bake Off looking?" asked Patrick, as he readied five waxed-paper wrappers for her order.

"Don't talk to me about it. Your mother is never going to speak to me again after she tastes my entry. How did the fish demo go?"

"Good. We ran out of recipe cards. Though it turned out one of the audience had an undiscovered allergy to lemon sole. They had to take him off to the first-aid tent." He handed her a paper bag, heavy with hog roast rolls. "Have you seen my mum anywhere? She wanted to try our special mustard sauce."

"Last I saw of her was in the demo tent, talking pastry with Bonvivant. Out of interest, what would I have to do to get you to steal or destroy my cake before your mother gets to taste it?"

"Sabotage?" Patrick raised an eyebrow.

"Think of it as for a good cause."

"No can do, I'm afraid. It's against the cheffing code. Thou Shalt Not Destroy Food."

PC Lucy sighed, took the bag in her arms and went off to feed her fellow constables.

Lunchtime was now in full swing, and Chef Maurice and Patrick had their hands full trying to keep up with the ravenous crowd, which was mostly made up of young families, retired residents from the nearby Cotswold villages, and a few couples on a romantic day out in the countryside. One couple in particular, her with flame-red hair, him with dark glasses and neatly groomed stubble, were currently drawing the crowd's attention by their prolonged make-out session in the hog roast queue. Such antics were met with disapproving stares from their fellow queuers, along with Chef Maurice, who felt that this behaviour did not display sufficient anticipation about their upcoming meal.

The sautéed scallop stand was also doing a brisk trade, but as Patrick had predicted earlier, their patrons had soon run up against the conundrum—common to many a buffet party—as to how to support a plate, wield a fork *and* hold on to your drink, which in today's case took the form of a large paper cup filled with the local pear cider.

"Has anyone seen Edith— I mean, Miss Caruthers?" said Angie, hurrying up to the hog roast stand, her round face flushed. "Or Rory? It's one o'clock now, and they're meant to be in the Bake Off tent getting ready, but the only judge I can find is Chef Elizabeth— Oh, wait, I tell a lie, there's Arthur over there . . ."

Arthur, who had been quietly shuffling his way along the sautéed scallop queue with his jacket collar turned up, looked over at Angie in annoyance.

"Traitor!" shouted Chef Maurice, brandishing the apple-sauce ladle. "No extra hog roast for you!"

"Ah, Angela, there you are," said Miss Caruthers, striding up behind Angie. There were splash marks on her long tartan skirt and she wore an expression of mild displeasure. "There are children playing unsupervised in the creek. I'm aware it's not deep up here, but even so, we roped off that area for a reason. Where *are* their parents?"

She appeared to notice Chef Maurice and Patrick for the first time. "Excellent work, gentlemen," she said, nodding at the long queue. "We really must get you up to the school for a demonstration and career talk, let the girls know what being a chef is all about."

"It would be a pleasure, *madame*," said Chef Maurice, though he had private doubts as to the sincerity of her request. The parents of Miss Caruthers' pupils paid hefty sums to send their offspring to the Lady Eleanor School for Girls, and would likely react with horror at the thought of their carefully nurtured daughters taking up the long hours and low pay of a career chef.

Miss Caruthers dipped a teaspoon (clean, Chef Maurice noted) into the bowl of Le Cochon Rouge's special mustard sauce. "Exquisite. My sister, Deirdre, took up mustard-making and pickling last year when she retired. I must send her a jar of this sometime. Now, come along, Angela, shouldn't we all be getting ready for the Bake Off?"

"I was just saying that I couldn't find the rest of— Ah, I see Rory over there," said Angie, waving frantically as she spotted her husband over on the far side of the field, deep in conversation with the M.P. for the Beakley and Endleby area. Karole the Research Rabbit stood nearby, shifting her weight from foot to foot, clearly regretting the choice of four-inch heels in a soft springtime field.

Eventually, Miss Caruthers and her team managed to corral all the judges into the Bake Off tent—all, that was, apart from Miranda Matthews. Angie and Tricia, the frizzy-haired treasurer of the Beakley Ladies' Institute, were dispatched to carry out a thorough search of the stalls and tents for the missing celebrity chef.

Every seat in the Bake Off tent was taken, and there was a sizable crowd milling around the edges. Chef Maurice shuffled his way over to the judges' table, where Miss Caruthers was surveying the crowd with pursed lips. They were already running three minutes behind schedule, and a few babies were getting fractious in the stuffy confines of the tent.

"Perhaps, *madame*, if you require a judge to stand in until Mademoiselle Miranda arrives?"

You could see the well-polished cogs turning beneath Miss Caruthers' smart grey curls. The recent surge in the popularity of baking television had led to a bumper crop of Bake Off entries, which were currently jostling for space on the creaking trestle table. It was a warm day, too, and Mayor Gifford in particular was already starting to look a tad overheated in his bunny suit. Perhaps there could be no harm in at least—

"Police! Someone call the police!" The cry came from the back of the tent, and Tricia stumbled into view, closely followed by Angie, her usual rosy complexion now milk white.

"What's happened?" said Miss Caruthers, rising magisterially and hurrying down the aisle.

"It— It's Miranda," spluttered Angie, running to meet her. "We just found her down by the creek. She— She's been drowned!"

CHAPTER 4

There was uproar in the Bake Off tent. Parents leapt to their feet, clutching their offspring, while the gaggle of local journalists threw aside their coffee cups and sprang into action.

PC Lucy, with a quick nod at PC Sara to follow her, made her way over to Angie and Tricia, who were both descending into babbling hysteria. A couple of the other constables, who had been standing at the back of the tent with hog roast rolls in their hands, stepped forward to calm the crowd back into their seats.

"Why? Why would someone do this?" cried Angie, while Tricia collapsed into Miss Caruthers' arms.

Near the front of the tent, there were gasps and shouts as a little girl, set off by the panic, ran head first into the long white tablecloth hanging off the Bake Off entries table, pulling the material with her as she went. Cakes, tarts and pastries came sliding over the edge, like a sugar-laden Niagara Falls. PC Lucy watched as her own cake executed a gentle forwards roll, then landed, seemingly unscathed, on the grass.

Drat, she thought, then shook herself. Now was not the time for worrying about baking. She turned her attention to the task of ushering Angie, Tricia and Miss Caruthers out of the tent.

"It was horrible," gulped Tricia, as PC Sara led her out into the open air. "How— How—"

"You better show us where you found her," said PC Lucy. "The rest of the team will be on their way. Miss Caruthers, if you'll let the others know where we've gone . . ."

The headmistress nodded and disappeared back into the tent.

"How could something like this happen?" Angie, still white, clutched at PC Lucy's arm. "Who would do something like this?"

PC Lucy opened her mouth to reply that it might just have been a terrible accident, they couldn't know anything yet, but a dull weight in her gut was telling her otherwise.

Either that, or she really shouldn't have ordered that second jumbo hog roll.

It was a fraught five minutes' walk along the tangled, overgrown path that led downstream alongside the drifting waters of Warren's Creek. This section of the woods, bordering on the Fayre-ground field, was marked as private property—though from the sight of the occasional crushed drinks can and chocolate bar wrapper, the moss-covered signs were not always obeyed by the local population.

There was a low higgledy-piggledy fence lining the edge of the woods, but even Angie, the shortest of the group and wearing a knee-length tweed skirt, was able to climb over without major fuss.

Following the stream, they eventually emerged into a clearing where a small jetty stood, poking out over the placid waters. It was an idyllic spot, sheltered by tall elms, with the grass spotted with white and purple crocuses, and bright daffodils lining the water's edge.

Idyllic, that was, save for the body floating face down in the shallow waters by the jetty.

Tricia and Angie quickly turned their backs, clinging together on the edge of the clearing.

"There's blood on the back of her head," said PC Sara in low tones. PC Lucy nodded.

"Did either of you touch or move the body?" she asked.

Angie shook her head, from behind a lace-edged handkerchief. "I tried to lean over and reach her, in case . . ." Her voice faltered. "But she was too far, and her head . . ."

"So then we ran all the way back to get someone," said Tricia.

"Did you pass anyone on your way, here or back? Anyone in the woods at all?"

Both women shook their heads.

Twigs cracked and leaves rustled as Mayor Gifford, looking as severe and authoritative as possible for a man wearing a pink bunny suit, appeared out of the woods,

45

closely followed by Miss Caruthers and PC Alistair. Miss Caruthers' thin-lipped frown and the pained look on PC Alistair's freckled face suggested that both had tried, and failed, to prevent the mayor from stomping down into the crime scene.

Mayor Gifford ran his gaze swiftly around the clearing, then turned on PC Lucy.

"Why have you dragged my wife down here? She could have just told you where to find the . . . this spot, no need to bring her down here to see it all again."

"It was best that Mrs Gifford and Mrs Walters showed us the site themselves. There's no need for the two of you to stay here now," she said, turning to Angie and Tricia, "but we'd please ask that you stay around at the Fayre so we can take your witness statements."

"Statements? Angie, don't you go answering any of their questions without me present, you hear?" growled Mayor Gifford.

"You're more than welcome to be there as well, Mr Gifford. It will just be some routine questions. Nothing out of the ordinary," she added, as Mayor Gifford's furry ears started to vibrate ominously.

Accompanied by PC Sara, the Giffords made their way back up the path, followed by Tricia and Miss Caruthers, leaving PC Lucy and Alistair to examine the scene before the rest of the team arrived.

"Could she have slipped and hit her head?" said PC Alistair, crouching down on the edge of the jetty.

"Possibly. It might have been enough to knock her out. Though it hasn't rained the whole of this week," said PC Lucy, running a hand over the dry wood. "And she's wearing trainers. Pretty hard to fall over in those." She pointed at Miranda's incongruously sporty footwear, then frowned.

Hadn't she seen Miranda teetering around on stage in some neon-coloured stiletto heels? Trainers, even purple ones with orange laces, didn't seem like they'd be Miranda's first choice for footwear, not even for a stroll in the woods.

She stood back up and stared around the clearing. The woods were dense in these parts, but even so, the perpetrator, whoever he or she was, would have been foolish to stick to the path by the creek—much better to cut through the woods straight up to the main road, where there were plenty of little lay-bys and turn-offs used by visitors who stopped to admire the Cotswold scenery. Easy to leave a car there, and sneak down here through the woods . . .

But she was getting ahead of herself. For now, the important thing was to have a good look around, before rain or trampling feet obscured any helpful hints of what had happened.

"So you reckon it might not have been an accident?" asked PC Alistair, now inspecting the construction of the little jetty.

PC Lucy, using a long branch to push away the foliage surrounding the path, stopped as something metallic caught her eye.

"Unfortunately," she said, "that scenario is looking less and less likely. Have a look at this."

PC Alistair scrambled up and hurried over. At their feet, half-hidden by the twisted brown leaves, was a short length of thick cast-iron pipe, the type used for old-fashioned plumbing. It was about the length of PC Lucy's forearm, and across one end was a shimmer of dark blood.

"So it was murder," breathed PC Alistair, who rather revelled in the stating of the obvious.

PC Lucy nodded. Someone out there, it seemed, had decided it was time for Miranda Matthews to hang up her apron.

For good.

CHAPTER 5

The cookery demonstration tent had been turned into an impromptu tea room for the distressed and detained. Arthur stood at the hobs, keeping an eye on two simmering pans of water, while Chef Maurice had managed to requisition a box of loose Darjeeling from the Gourmet Tea Leaf stand, as well as a stack of white mugs, as yet undefaced, from the Paint-Your-Mug stall.

Arthur had suspicions that his friend's sudden tea-providing tendencies had less to do with altruism, and more to do with achieving a suitable eavesdropping proximity to the key crime scene witnesses, who were currently sat on folding chairs in a little semicircle around PC Lucy.

"So tell me what happened when you first went looking for Miranda," she was saying, notebook held at the ready.

Tricia hiccupped into a tissue. "First, we had a quick look around the stalls and in all the tents. We thought she'd just forgotten the time. We also tried her dressing room—"

"She had a dressing room? Where was this?"

"It's just a little tent, round the back of here," said Angie. "She wanted somewhere to get ready, keep a change of outfit, that kind of thing."

"Okay. And then?"

"Well, she wasn't there, so then we thought she might have gone for a walk. It's ever so pretty around here this time of year," said Tricia. "We went down to the bit of the creek at the end of the field, where all the kiddies were playing, but she wasn't there."

"So then we just followed the path," said Angie, "down to where we . . . well, you know . . ." She broke off with a shiver.

"What made you think Miranda would have followed the path into private land? It's not exactly the most obvious place to go walking," said PC Lucy.

Mayor Gifford, sitting beside his wife with one furry paw across her shoulder, looked up sharply, clearly unhappy at the tone of conversation.

Angie looked startled. "Oh! I didn't even think about that. You see"—she looked over at Miss Caruthers—"that bit of the woods belongs to the school. In fact, the creek runs all the way through our land. The girls go walking up and down there all the time in the summer—"

She stopped with a look of horror on her face.

"Not to worry, Mrs Gifford," said PC Lucy. "My colleagues will have roped off the area already. I'll make sure someone telephones the school to let them know, of course. But I still don't see—"

"Miranda Matthews was a pupil at Lady Eleanor, some

twenty years ago now," explained Miss Caruthers. "The same year as Angela, if I recall correctly."

Angie nodded.

"So you're saying she would have known this area well? Including the path along the creek?"

"It wouldn't surprise me if she remembered," said Miss Caruthers. "It's a lovely stretch of woodland, even if our groundskeeper doesn't tend to the path quite as much as he did in earlier years."

There was a pause in proceedings as Arthur and Chef Maurice approached with trays to distribute steaming mugs of tea—and to get within better earshot of the questioning.

PC Lucy waved away the proffered mug. "So when was the last time you all saw Miranda? Alive, I mean."

"The last time I saw her was at the end of her cookery demonstration," said Miss Caruthers.

"Me too," said Tricia.

PC Lucy consulted a flyer. "And that finished at twelve thirty, correct?"

The Spring Fayre Committee ladies all nodded.

"I last saw her in her dressing tent, right afterwards," said Angie. "I popped my head in to see if she wanted anything to eat, but she said she wasn't hungry."

"Can you recall what type of shoes Miranda was wearing when you saw her?"

Angie looked puzzled. "I don't remember. The same ones she was wearing earlier, I would have thought. Pink high heels."

"And did Miranda mention anything about going for a walk? Or meeting someone during lunchtime?"

"She didn't say anything to me." Angie paused. "I mean, now that I think about it, she was a bit, well, distracted. And she was a bit short, like maybe she wanted to be left alone. But she gets like that sometimes, especially after a big event. It's never anything personal," she added generously.

"What about you, Mr Gifford?" asked PC Lucy. "When did you last see Miranda Matthews?"

"Eh? Can't say I paid her much attention, cooking's not really my thing, you know. Saw her signing some autographs earlier in the morning. Long before lunchtime, though. Can't help you there, I'm afraid."

"Arthur? Maurice?" said PC Lucy, looking over at her two spectators, who had settled themselves into folding chairs not far away.

Arthur shook his head. "I stayed for her demo, but didn't see her after that."

"I left before, when Mademoiselle Miranda started her cake covered in the Smarties. *C'est un sacrilège*, to claim that such a cake is a—"

"Yes, yes, thank you both for your input," said PC Lucy quickly. She looked down at her notes. "So Miranda was last seen by Mrs Gifford, who spoke to her in her tent after the demo. We'll put out a call for information, see if anyone saw her leaving her tent, or passed her walking down to the creek."

"You'll be keeping my wife's name out of this, I assume?" said Mayor Gifford, with a cross look at Angie.

"We will. But I have to warn you, I'd be surprised if the local press don't try contacting Mrs Gifford and Mrs Walters in the meantime. They were all in the Bake Off tent when . . . the incident was reported. Of course, there's no obligation on your part to speak to them," she added, looking towards Angie and Tricia.

"I should bloody well think not!" snapped Mayor Gifford, while Angie nodded meekly.

Questioning over, Miss Caruthers left to drive Tricia home, while the mayor led PC Lucy over to a corner of the tent for an angry discourse on the abuse of police power and the so-called freedoms of the press, which PC Lucy listened to with an expression of blank official politeness.

Angie collected up the finished tea mugs and brought them over to the sink area.

"You can put them down there," said Arthur, pointing one pink-rubber-gloved elbow at the counter nearby. "Apparently"—he shot a look at Chef Maurice—"I'm the designated pot wash for the day."

"As the English say, if the glove fits . . ." Chef Maurice sipped happily at his own mug, held in one XL-sized fist.

Angie twisted the end of her chiffon scarf around her fingers and threw a nervous look back at her husband, who was still busy berating the stone-faced PC Lucy.

"I was wondering, Mr Maurice . . ."

"*Oui, madame?*"

"Well, I remember hearing about—"

She got no further, though, as the sound of her own name was bellowed across the room. "I— Never mind, I better go. Rory's calling for me. Thank you for the tea."

She hurried off.

"I wonder what that was all about," said Arthur.

"Do not worry, *mon ami*. I am sure that we will discover more as we make an inspection of the matter."

"The matter? What matter?"

Chef Maurice threw his hands in the air. "There has been the murder of a chef, and you ask me what matter? This is a most serious happening!"

"So Miranda Matthews is now a chef?"

"Bah, the public, they do not make a difference between myself"—he thumped his chest—"and the type of Miranda Matthews. To them, she is a chef. So we must ask if other chefs, too, are in danger from this murderer."

Arthur gave this statement its due consideration. As an entirely spurious reason for Chef Maurice to indulge in his penchant for dabbling in crime investigation, he could, Arthur supposed, have done a lot worse.

"You might be on to something there, old chap," said Arthur, as they wandered out through the now-deserted Fayre-ground stalls. "For all we know, there might be some serial killer on the loose with a predilection for bumping off famous chefs."

"Ah, so you agree that this case is one requiring of our attention?"

Arthur wasn't too sure about this part, but he conceded that it couldn't hurt to make a few enquiries of their own. Thankfully, he pointed out, if the serial-killer-famous-chef theory was correct, it meant that Chef Maurice would be well clear of any danger.

They headed back up the lane into the village with Chef Maurice striding on ahead, nose in the air, wearing an expression of injuriously injured pride.

That evening, the staff of Le Cochon Rouge sat down at the big kitchen table to tuck into plates of grilled sardines on toasted seeded bread, to fortify themselves for the busy dinner service ahead. Many of the Spring Fayre visitors had decided to soothe their frayed nerves with a slap-up dinner before the drive home, and the restaurant was fully booked. The kitchen crew were joined at the table by Mrs Merland, who had offered to pitch in with a special dessert for the evening menu.

"Have they found the murderer yet?" asked Alf, pouring some balsamic vinaigrette over his sardines.

"This one'll have 'em stumped for a while, I'll bet," said Dorothy, nodding in satisfaction at the prospect of weeks of speculation and idle gossip with her regular customers. "Big crowd, no witnesses, all 'em woods just to disappear into. You know it was all on the telly this afternoon? We made the national news, we did."

Patrick nodded, though he didn't quite share their head waitress's level of enthusiasm. He wondered how the next few weeks' table bookings were going to fare, though he had to admit that the news report had painted the village of Beakley in quite a flattering light. If you ignored the part about brutal murder, of course.

"Makes you think twice about wandering about late at night," continued Dorothy.

"But it happened right in the middle of the day," Patrick pointed out.

"All the more reason to know how to defend yourself," replied Dorothy. She had recently signed up to a series of self-defence classes run by Mrs Petticoat, the vicar's wife. However, it seemed that Mrs Petticoat was a subscriber to the belief that the best defence was a good offence, and news of Dorothy's one-inch punch had spread fast through the village. Tips had more than doubled over the last month alone.

Chef Maurice, who generally found that the application of a heavy steel-capped toe was usually enough to ward off any would-be attacker, shook his head. "It is possible that the attack on Mademoiselle Miranda may not have been a random chance."

"Cor!" said Alf. "Like, someone had some kind of vain debtor against her?"

They looked at him.

"I think you mean a 'vendetta'," said Patrick, after a few moments.

Alf was currently going through a mafia movie phase, which had led to various recent attempts to tough talk the vegetable box into submission when he thought no one else was around. Still, it provided some light relief in a demanding schedule, given that the job of commis chef mostly consisted of following orders that could not be refused.

"I am grieved, Madame Merland, that you have travelled all this way to be welcomed by such a tragedy," said Chef Maurice, tearing off another chunk of bread.

"Not at all," replied Mrs Merland. "First chance I've had to get out of the kitchens in quite a while. And I have to admit, I did have another reason for coming down here." She turned to smile at Patrick, who felt a surge of sudden alarm. The Merlands were not a family given to overt displays of familial affection. Either the years had finally begun to soften his mother's no-nonsense approach to parenting, or something was afoot . . .

Mrs Merland laid her hands flat on the table. "I'll get straight to the point, no use beating around the bush in these circumstances."

An icy chill grasped Patrick's chest. There had been a throwaway remark the other day about a routine health check-up, but surely—

"I've found a manor house up in the North Lakes, just outside Buttermere. Georgian build, in good repair, superb views, and the best thing is that it's already being run as a restaurant, so no problems with the local council there. I'm proposing to do the place up, turn the upstairs floors into guest bedrooms, and reopen it as a hotel and restaurant."

"Sounds lovely," said Dorothy.

"*Oui*, but much work," said Chef Maurice, who had firm views on the notion of combining gastronomy and the garrisoning of the guests afterwards—in short, that the whole endeavour was more trouble than it ever could possibly be worth. For one thing, it involved waking up at unseemly hours in order to provide said guests with breakfast, which was an insult in itself, as any sensible person knew that the best way to appreciate an evening of fine dining was to sleep it off until at least midday the day after.

"And," said Mrs Merland, "I want Patrick to join me up there as head chef."

A blanket of silence thudded down, like thick snow off a cabin roof.

Chef Maurice was the first to recover. "But that is *impossible*! Patrick is already my sous-chef here. I will not allow it!"

Mrs Merland turned to Patrick. "If you accept, you'll be an equity holder, along with myself and your father. You choose your team, of course. I'll head up the pastry side, as well as overseeing the hotel management. I need to sign the lease in five days' time."

Patrick opened his mouth, but nothing came out.

"I know this is all a bit irregular," continued Mrs Merland, "but I thought Maurice deserved to know exactly what offer I'm putting on the table. Take your time to think it over, of course."

"Time? To *think*?" Chef Maurice leapt up from the table. "This is *incroyable*! To come here into my kitchen and attempt to steal my sous-chef—"

"He's my son, too, you know," said Mrs Merland mildly.

"Bah!" came the reply, in tones that suggested the miracle of childbirth held nothing in comparison to the task of training up a competent sous-chef. "Patrick, what is it that you say to all this?"

"Whuh?" Patrick looked up. "You don't expect me to give you an answer right here and now, do you?"

"Of course not, dear," said Mrs Merland, touching his hand, while Chef Maurice spluttered as he struggled to breathe in and swear loudly in French at the same time. "I'd better be getting back to my B&B. The hazelnut dacquoise cake is chilling in the walk-in. It just needs slicing. I'll pop by tomorrow to say goodbye before my train."

Then she was gone.

"That woman!" Chef Maurice waved his fist at the door. "She is a . . . a . . ."

"Now, now, there, we don't want to be saying anything we'll be regretting later," said Dorothy, rolling up her sleeves just in case she'd need to jujitsu armlock her boss if things went downhill.

"Humph! Then she has thrown down the metal glove. And I accept her challenge!" With that, Chef Maurice grabbed his hat and stormed out of the back door.

"Cor, a job as head chef. Not bad, eh?" said Alf, with a nervous look at Patrick.

"It's like they don't think I even get a say in the matter," said Patrick, staring at the back door.

"I thought your mum said—"

"Sure, she says things like 'take your time', but you can tell she doesn't expect me to think twice about it."

"So whatcha think you'll do?"

"Not a clue." Patrick was still fuming at the presumptuousness of it all; Chef Maurice assuming his loyal sous-chef would never think to leave, and his mother just as certain her son would jump at the chance to join her venture. Maybe it would teach them all a lesson if he just went and upped sticks to Outer Mongolia.

He wondered if it was possible to make a decent *crème anglaise* using yak's milk . . .

"I do hope chef's not gone off to do anything silly," said Dorothy, piling up the finished plates.

"Probably just walking around out there, sulking," said Patrick.

Unfortunately, what they'd all forgotten was that Chef Maurice was not a single-track sulker. He could sulk and get up to all kinds of trouble, all at the same time.

So while Patrick and Alf fired up the hobs in preparation for dinner service, a little red Citroën reversed itself around in the yard, spraying up gravel all around, and headed out into the dusky evening.

Its mission: staff retention. By any means possible.

* * *

Being the only two female police officers in the Cowton and Beakley Constabulary had left PC Lucy and PC Sara with two apparent choices: to become the best of friends, or each other's prime nemesis. Both being women of a sound, practical nature, they'd promptly opted for the former.

Tonight, they were the only ones left in the office, along with an empty extra-large takeaway pizza box. PC Sara sat at her computer, scanning through the hundreds of photographs from the Fayre, requisitioned from the local journalists (also probably working late tonight), while PC Lucy was engaged in the laborious task of combing through Miranda Matthews' phone records.

"Nothing much here," said PC Lucy, tossing the final sheet onto her desk. "The only call she made this morning was to a local taxi company. And the week before, it's mostly just been calls to and from her agent, and Angela Gifford. A few to some local restaurants, and one to Cowton Country Property Lettings. I'll look into that last one when they're open tomorrow. There's one missed call from this morning, just before ten, from an unregistered mobile number, but she didn't call them back. I'll try to get the number traced."

"Any voicemails?"

"Nope. How's the photo trawling?"

"Plenty of Miranda up until and during her cookery demo." PC Sara flipped her screen round to face PC Lucy. "Now *that's* what I call a celebration cake," she added, pointing at the photo of a glossy multi-coloured creation on a cake stand, with Miranda posing chirpily behind.

"I saw that part of the demo. She just covered a sponge cake in Smarties and then blowtorched the whole thing. Not exactly difficult."

"Says the girlfriend of a gourmet chef. Never forget, I still knew you back in the days when you thought mascarpone was a type of Italian horse."

"Very funny. Any sign of Miranda after the demo?"

PC Sara shook her head. "But you were right about the shoes," she said, tapping the screen. "She was definitely wearing pink high heels when she left the demo tent."

"Which puts paid to the theory she was attacked in her dressing tent and carried all the way to the creek. No attacker would bother changing her shoes."

"Unless she was attacked just after she put on the trainers."

"And still carried several hundred metres down to Warren's Creek, along with a piece of blood-covered piping? All without being seen?" PC Lucy shook her head. "Far more likely she changed and sneaked down there herself. The back of her tent faced the woodlands, she could have easily got out that way."

"Meeting someone?"

"A possibility."

PC Sara scrolled onwards. "Honestly, who turns up to a family fair dressed like a pin-up bunny?" She waved her hand at the photos on-screen, in which one particular journalist had decided to express his admiration of Miss Karole Linton's exquisitely sculpted derrière by taking several close-up pictures of it.

"Maybe Mayor Gifford snagged the last proper bunny suit at the store," suggested PC Lucy.

"Even so, no need for her to go around flaunting like that," sniffed PC Sara.

PC Lucy raised an eyebrow. Her friend was not exactly the shy type when it came to squeezing herself into skintight leather leggings and the occasional dangerously low-cut top. In fact, if PC Sara's perennial crackpot diets ever succeeded in shifting the magical, and frankly invisible, 'last ten pounds' that she claimed were keeping her from an appearance down at the local swimming pool, PC Lucy had no doubts that her friend would be more than happy to take up the role of Easter Bunny Girl at the next opportunity.

"Now, here's a man who looks good in pink," said PC Sara. She expanded a photo of Mayor Gifford, standing with one paw around Mr Whittaker, the deputy mayor, and the other clasping the shoulders of Mr Kabilt, M.P. for the neighbouring constituency.

"He does?" Of course, PC Lucy had grudgingly admired Mayor Gifford's achievements over the last few years in cleaning up Cowton's High Street and opening the new sports centre, conveniently located only a few minutes' walk from the police station. But she'd never given much thought to the mayor's apparent attraction when it came to the female vote.

"It's the shoulders," said PC Sara. "Everyone likes a man with good shoulders."

"Shoulders or no shoulders, it's no excuse for him being a right royal pain this afternoon." It seemed to her that Mayor Gifford had taken the murder as something of a personal affront. Perhaps he'd had plans to make use of Miranda's telegenic presence as part of his political campaign, and was now feeling unjustly thwarted.

"Bah! The English, why is it they love so much the dressing up?" came a familiar voice from behind them. "They dress as animals, as robots, as spacemen. The men dress as women, the women dress as the men. I saw once a man run a race dressed as a teapot!" Clearly, competing in a sports event in the guise of the nation's favourite beverage constituted a grave offence in the eyes of Chef Maurice.

"Maurice, this is a police station. You can't just barge into the office whenever you want. Are you reporting a crime?"

Chef Maurice sank down into PC Alistair's empty chair and swept off his hat. "There has been *un désastre* at the restaurant!"

"Really?"

By now, PC Lucy was more than familiar with Chef Maurice's idea of what constituted a disaster. Just last month, he'd called up the station in a fury, insisting that one of his customers must be stealing all the restaurant's teaspoons. A search of the chef's own laundry hamper, however, had unveiled no less than four dozen spoons, buried and forgotten in various pockets, and five more tucked into the lining of his tall white chef's hat. "In case of emergency," had been his defence.

"*Oui*. I come to warn you, *mademoiselle*, that Patrick faces a most grave danger." Voice brimming with indignation, he proceeded to outline Mrs Merland's catastrophic offer.

"And what has Patrick said?" asked PC Lucy, her stomach doing a little flip.

"He says nothing! He sits there, silent as the lamb! You must talk to him, *mademoiselle*, and make him see the sense. Even if you must use"—an alarming eyebrow waggle was here employed—"every means available to you."

PC Lucy glared at him, though she wondered if she should be flattered or insulted by the chef's insinuation about her special powers of persuasion.

"Maurice, you know as well as I do, this decision is entirely up to Patrick. It's not for us to make his career choices for him."

Chef Maurice looked perplexed at this last statement.

"Then you will not help?" he said finally, in injured tones.

There was the clatter of the office door, a loud squelching sound, then PC Alistair waddled in, wearing a pair of long rubber waders approximately five times too big for him.

"We've been dredging the creek all evening, miss— Uh, I mean, PC Gavistone. And look what we dug up!" He held up a plastic bag containing a mud-covered digital camera, the type with a long, fat lens and more buttons than a clown costume factory. It was attached to a dangling leather case and strap. "Doesn't look like it had been down there long. Though we can't get it to turn on."

"Any idea where it came from?" asked PC Sara.

"Better than that," said PC Alistair. He pressed on the plastic, smoothing away the mud from the leather casing, to reveal two gold-embossed initials: M.M.

"Reckon she had it with her when she was attacked and dropped it?" said PC Sara to PC Lucy. "Or threw it in herself?"

"Hmm. If she wanted to get rid of the contents, surely it would have been easier to just wipe the memory card. I'd put my money on the first idea. Might even be that this is what her attacker was after." She pushed the plastic bag back towards PC Alistair. "Find someone who can get the pictures off this thing. And then"—she wrinkled her nose—"go home and shower. Please."

"Right you are, miss!"

As Alistair squelched back out of the door, PC Lucy realised they'd not heard a peep out of Chef Maurice in the last few minutes.

Sure enough, she turned around to find him sat in PC Sara's chair, index finger jabbing at the keyboard as he scrolled through the photos from the Fayre.

"Ah, this is a thing of beauty, is it not?" He crossed his arms over his chest, beaming with pride at a close-up shot of a mustard-slathered hog roast roll.

PC Lucy finally managed to dislodge the chef, after promising to contact the photographer and get him a copy of the photo, and also agreeing to speak to Patrick regarding his future career choice.

"Just as a sounding board," she warned. "It's still his decision, I'm not going to go taking sides."

After all, common wisdom dictated that the best way to make a man do what you wanted was to appear utterly indifferent to whichever option he chose.

Plus, she had a high-profile murder investigation to be getting on with. She thought about PC Alistair's latest find. She was no expert, but that camera looked like a piece of pro equipment. What had Miranda been doing with it? Why had she taken it with her on her walk along Warren's Creek?

And, should they manage to salvage its contents, what might the photographs show?

CHAPTER 6

The next day brought the usual horde of Sunday lunchers to the low-slung oak-beamed dining room of Le Cochon Rouge, and Chef Maurice and his team had their hands full rushing out plates of roast sirloin beef served with fluffy Yorkshire puddings, accompanied by pots of home-made horseradish sauce and an armada of gravy boats.

In the kitchens, head chef, sous-chef and commis chef moved fast and furiously in the quasi-choreographed synchrony of a well-tuned kitchen. But if one watched carefully, it was just possible to detect a touch of frost in the air between the head chef and his sous.

"Where's the salt got to?" Patrick glanced around, his tea-towelled hand gripping a griddle pan of pork chops, boldly criss-crossed with sizzling char marks. "Chef, can you pass the salt?"

"*Comment?*" Chef Maurice looked up from slicing yet another joint of sirloin. A perfectly even tranche of moist, just-pink beef fell to the chopping board as he spoke. "Hah, you think you are ready to be a head chef—that you are, as they say, worth the salt! And yet, you cannot even find it?"

Patrick sighed, walked over and grabbed the stainless steel tub from beside his boss's elbow.

Chef Maurice tut-tutted. "Alf, the roast potatoes. They are in?"

"*Oui*, chef!" Alf, tipped a pot of boiled potatoes into a sizzling tray of goose fat, shoved it back into the oven and slammed the door. "How comes people always say someone is 'worth their salt', anyway?"

"Humph," said Chef Maurice, now tonging a generous three slices of beef onto each waiting plate. "It is because of the English and their idiots."

"You mean idioms," said Patrick. "It's not the English who have idiots." This last part was muttered under his breath.

"Aha, I have the answer." Chef Maurice jabbed his tongs in the air, like an orchestra conductor struck with a good idea. "It is because salt brings out the best flavour in a dish, but it cannot improve a dish that is already bad. So a man who is worth his salt, is one who already has worth!"

At that thought, he grabbed the salt tub back off Patrick.

"A more common theory," said Patrick, "is that it comes from how the Romans used to pay their soldiers in salt, because it was so valuable back then. It's where the word 'salary' comes from, too."

"Cor," said Alf, giving the tub of salt a look of newfound respect. Then he frowned. "So what did they do when it rained and their salt got all wet? Wouldn't it just disappear?"

"Good question," said Patrick, with the faintly worried look of a man who has suddenly had his long-held beliefs put to the test.

"The Roman soldiers," said Chef Maurice, slicing away, "also had the most grave punishments for those who deserted their armies."

He moved off to check on the latest batch of Yorkshire puddings, and that was the end of that discussion.

Aside from the busy reservations diary, Chef Maurice had another reason for putting his nascent murder case on a brief hold. The important thing about crime investigation, he knew, especially the bits requiring the somewhat illegal entering of a property that did not belong to you, was to always make sure to take along a friend. Ideally one who could not run as fast as you.

Arthur, currently up in London at a food writing symposium, fitted this role abundantly well, so it wasn't until the Monday morning after that the two friends could be found loitering across the street from the doorway leading up to Miranda Matthews' flat, which occupied the space above a milliner's shop on Cowton's High Street.

The door was open, but the yellow-and-blue-checked police car pulled up on the curb outside was currently deterring any move on their part.

"So what exactly are we planning to do once the police

finish their business up there?" said Arthur. "It's not like they're going to hand us the keys as they leave."

"Ah, do not worry. When you were away just now to buy the coffee, I went to make some preparations." Chef Maurice adjusted his pork-pie hat, the one he kept for special outings, and blew on his styrofoam cup of black coffee. "Now, we simply wait."

Arthur decided it was best not to ask his friend what these preparations had entailed. When one spent any length of time around Chef Maurice, one soon learnt that plausible deniability was a good position to be able to maintain.

"Don't you think we should have started off talking to people who knew Miranda? Instead of indulging in a light spot of breaking and entering?"

"Bah. People, they can lie. But to see a person's home, it is like stepping into the soul of the owner. The house, it is an Englishman's castle, is it not?"

"Yes, and that's why we don't go around mounting attacks on those belonging to other people." Across the street, the police were filing out down the narrow staircase. Thankfully for Arthur and Chef Maurice, PC Lucy was not amongst their number—she would certainly have questioned their motive for standing around drinking takeaway coffee in the High Street at ten in the morning— but they did catch a glimpse of PC Alistair, struggling down the steps carrying an overflowing box of papers and a laptop.

The door thudded shut behind the policemen, who then climbed into their car and made a quick departure, accompanied by a spurt of sirens.

"*Allons-y!* The investigation, it begins." Chef Maurice lost no time in hurrying across the road, narrowly missing an altercation with one of the trundling local buses. At Miranda's front door, he looked around carefully, then drew a teaspoon out from his jacket and jabbed it into the gap between the doorframe and lock. The door popped open.

"How the—?"

Arthur leaned in closer. A wine cork (stamped, he noticed, with the name of one of the more exclusive Burgundian *domaines*) had been wedged into the rect-angular metal opening where the lock catch would normally sit.

"Where the heck did you learn to do that?" he asked, as they shuffled quickly into the cramped hallway and closed the door behind them.

"Ah, I saw it in a detective programme last year. It was fortunate that the lock here was of a similar construction."

The narrow staircase leading up to Miranda Matthews' flat was dark and slightly dingy, a complete contrast to the architectural marvel above. It was a bright, airy space, spanning the width of the two shops below, with a line of sash windows facing the street and letting in the warm spring sunshine. The floors were washed oak, resembling the pale grey of an upmarket beach hut, and the walls were painted a subtle yet luxurious shade of off-white. The furniture was modern but comfortable, all soft curves and polished wood surfaces.

"Bit of a fan of wildlife photography, it seems," said Arthur, admiring a series of framed black-and-white prints, each featuring a dramatic close-up animal portrait. A pensive gorilla knitted his brows at the camera, a toothy lioness yawned in the dusty shade, and a giraffe stood staring regally out across a sunset plain. "Isn't that a Western lowland gorilla?" he added, having recently watched a documentary on the subject. "Of the genus *gorilla*, species *gorilla*, subspecies *gorilla*?"

Chef Maurice, who usually confined his interest in the animal kingdom to the more edible species, rubbed his moustache. "The *Gorilla gorilla gorilla*?"

"Afraid so."

"*Interessant.*"

In the open-plan kitchen, which was of course kitted out with all the latest culinary mod-cons, Arthur's gaze was drawn to the blown-up magazine cover shoot hung up by the window. It showed a twenty-something-year-old Miranda, arms linked cheerfully with a young woman with flame-red wavy hair. They both wore pastel-coloured aprons and flirty smiles aimed at the camera.

"Gosh, that brings back memories. *Cook It Right!* Prime Saturday night TV—I remember Meryl making us watch it every week. Always wondered what happened to that other girl. What was her name, Gaby something-or-other?"

Chef Maurice, who was busy rummaging through the kitchen cupboards, shrugged.

"She got booted off the show pretty early, I recall. Got mixed up in some kind of scandal."

"Scandal?" Chef Maurice looked up from sniffing a jar of artichokes that he'd found in the fridge. He shook his head sadly at the rest of its contents, which consisted of several bottles of sparkling water, a jar of pasta sauce, and a brown-edged lettuce. A chef's fridge it was not.

"Yes, I think it might have been to do with drugs. Or something shady going on with one of the producers. I'm sure we could find out, if we need."

"Hmm, we will see." The lettuce was duly consigned to the rubbish chute, and they migrated into one of the bedrooms, which had been converted into a spacious home office. A glass-topped desk was covered in stacks of folders and papers, all showing the hand-sketched logo of a little thatched roof and the words below: 'The Little Cowton Kitchen'. There were also printouts of kitchen layouts, equipment purchase lists and class timing plans.

"Mademoiselle Miranda was to open a school of *cookery?*" said Chef Maurice, in the same manner as one just informed that Cruella de Vil was toying with the idea of opening a dog-grooming parlour.

"Well—" started Arthur, but further comment was curtailed by the sound of the door clicking shut downstairs and the thump of rising footsteps.

"Quick, *mon ami*! This could be the murderer, returning

to destroy the evidence. We must hide and observe." With that, Chef Maurice launched himself into the nearby closet.

Arthur looked around frantically. Miranda's office did not appear to offer many choices when it came to bodily concealment. Hiding under a glass desk definitely wouldn't win him the 'Camouflage of the Year' award. There would have been the standing-behind-the-door option, except that Miranda had installed sliding doors throughout the flat. As for the wardrobe, the clatter of hangers from inside indicated that Chef Maurice was already more than fully occupying the space within.

The footsteps had now reached the living room.

Chef Maurice stuck his head out of the wardrobe. "Why do you not hide? We must not be discovered!"

"Easy for you to say," hissed Arthur, eying up the bookcase in the corner. Perhaps if he shifted it forward a tad . . .

He had just managed to wedge half a hip and an entire leg behind the thing, when he heard a sharp intake of breath behind him.

"Mr Wordington-Smythe! What on earth are you doing with that bookcase?"

"Delivery for the kitchen," announced Dorothy, moving aside to allow through a blue-overalled man wheeling a waist-high cardboard box.

"Sign here, sir." A weathered clipboard was thrust under Patrick's nose.

Once the man was gone, Patrick and Alf circled the box warily, looking for any hint as to its contents. One could never tell what odd ingredient or item might have last caught their head chef's eye. Last month it had been a pair of life-sized stone pigs, which now stood guard outside the front door of Le Cochon Rouge, one of them wearing a flowerpot on its head.

Unfortunately, this box was simply labelled as for the attention of 'Le Cochon Rouge, Beakley', with a return address of some Lincolnshire business park.

Alf tapped a wooden spoon against the side, ears cocked.

"I don't think it's going to bite you, luv," said Dorothy, watching the antics of the two chefs, hands on hips.

"That's what chef said about those spider crabs last week," said Alf. The crustaceans that passed through their kitchens seemed to always have a bit of a soft spot for the young commis chef—or at least an unerring ability to find his soft spots, and pinch down hard on them.

"Better get this open, then. Might be something perishable." Patrick grabbed a paring knife and slit open the top of the box. A shiny leaflet fluttered down at his feet.

The logo looked tantalisingly familiar.

Surely it couldn't be . . .

He quickly cut away the rest of the cardboard.

"Cor!" said Alf, mouth agape in wonderment. Then he looked at Patrick. "So what is it?"

Their kitchen newcomer was a large, gleaming contraption, made of stainless steel, adorned with a row of dials with complicated-looking pictograms, and rather resembling the result of an illicit encounter between a food blender and a galactic spacecraft.

"It's a brand-new TM5000 Deluxe Professional ThermoMash," said Patrick, in awed tones. "It can do practically *anything*. It chops, stews, mashes, makes ice cream, stocks, bread, cheese. Apparently you can set it to make a perfect hollandaise in ten seconds flat."

"Humph, don't see what's so impressive about *that*," said Alf, crossing his arms and glaring at the machine with the look of a man whose job prospects are suddenly under threat.

"I've been on at chef to get us one of these for *months*. I wonder what made him suddenly—" Patrick stopped.

Dorothy, who hadn't worked this many years alongside chefs without developing an acute sense of self-preservation, chose this moment to nip away into the dining room, mumbling something about the napkins needing another ironing.

"Alf?" said Patrick.

"Er, yes?"

"When exactly did chef put in this order?"

"Um . . . Might have been after you left last night. I might have showed him how to order one on the Internet."

"*Might* have?"

"Um . . ."

77

Despite his escalating feelings of exasperation, Patrick had to admit he was also rather impressed. Chef Maurice must *really* want him to stay, to have been willing to set foot within two metres of a computer monitor.

(It wasn't that the head chef was I.T.-illiterate; one could consider him as more techno-embattled, waging a constant war with the electronic devices in his life. The attempted use of an electronic alarm clock had resulted in several mornings of unintentional 3 a.m. starts—which had been accompanied by a series of predawn phone calls to the rest of his kitchen staff, demanding to know why they had yet to turn up to work. His ancient mobile phone appeared only able to dial the Croatian talking clock, and the robotic vacuum cleaner, bought for him one Christmas by an optimistic Meryl, had managed on its first day to get into his chest of drawers and consume all his socks.)

However, even in the face of his head chef's techno-logical efforts, Patrick was determined to be a man unswayed by such means of persuasion.

"We're sending it back," he said firmly.

"We are?" said Alf, in hopeful tones.

"I'm not having chef think he can bribe me into staying. It's my decision, and I'm perfectly capable of making it without the help of a TM Professional—"

"—Deluxe Professional—"

"—*Deluxe* Professional ThermoMash. With the extra pasta-rolling attachment, too," sighed Patrick, tucking the leaflet back in amongst the stainless steel rotors.

Despite his claims to the contrary, he was aware that he was still no closer to making any decision than he'd been last night, when his mother had dropped her manor-house-sized bombshell on them all.

He'd been back and forth with himself on the merits of the new venture—his first head chef position, the chance to make a name for himself—and the downsides—starting life yet again in another village, and the prospect of Chef Maurice chasing him all around Beakley with a frying pan if he handed in his resignation. And then, of course, there was Lucy to think about. The Lake District was by no means an easy commute from the Cotswolds, and what with them both working long shifts and irregular hours . . .

Still, Patrick was looking forward to being able to discuss the whole matter with someone more sane than his current kitchen compatriots. Of course, he fully expected his girlfriend to drop the occasional heavy hint that she wanted him to stay—that was only natural.

But PC Lucy had a sound, level head, and he had a feeling she'd be infinitely more helpful when it came to thinking through his decision than a crazed French chef with a suddenly very large budget for culinary equipment.

Back at Miranda Matthews' flat, it took a while to persuade Angie Gifford that the *England Observer*'s food critic had not, in fact, been attempting to steal Miranda's solid-walnut bookcase, but instead had merely been trying to conceal himself behind said item in case she, Angie Gifford, had turned out to be a lead-pipe-wielding attacker.

Angie looked less than convinced, too, at the explanation that the two of them had simply stepped inside the flat after noticing the front door left unlocked, and, being good Cotswolds neighbours, had wanted to check that nothing had been taken.

"We might ask you the question, Madame Gifford, why *you* also are found here in the flat of Mademoiselle Miranda," said Chef Maurice sternly, having now left the confines of his wardrobe hideout. (A sudden appearance, it should be noted, that had not done much to soothe Angie Gifford's already frazzled nerves.)

"Miranda left me a set of her keys when she first moved in, as I was the only person she knew around here. The police told me they were coming this morning, so I wanted to pop in and check they hadn't made a mess of things. And pick up some of the paperwork for the cookery school." She indicated the brochures on the desk.

"You knew of these plans of Mademoiselle Miranda?"

"Of course, it was our project together," said Angie, oblivious to Chef Maurice's look of moustache-quivering indignation. She ran a hand across a glossy flyer. "We weren't going to tell anyone yet, seeing as we hadn't secured the site. And I didn't want anyone at Lady Eleanor to know I was thinking of leaving. I'm afraid some of the other teachers are a bit stuck in their ways. They treat it as a huge scandal whenever someone leaves to go to another school, let alone thinks about doing something like this."

"Other teachers such as Madame Caruthers, for example?"

"Oh, yes, I dread to think what she'd have said to me. Not that she'll even be around next year—she's retiring this summer, you know—but teaching's been her whole life. She simply can't understand anyone wanting to do anything *different*."

"But you'd still be teaching cookery, wouldn't you?" said Arthur.

Angie gave a little sigh. "If only Edith would see it like that. But I can just imagine her, complaining that all we'd be doing is catering to pampered housewives. But we had all kinds of plans, running subsidised classes for young parents, setting up a Sunday charity kitchen, that sort of thing. It wasn't all going to be cupcakes."

"You speak, *madame*, as if your cookery school will no longer take place."

Angie stared down at the brochure, open at a picture of herself and Miranda posing in front of an old-fashioned stove. "I don't see how it can, now. You see, it was Miranda who was going to provide the financing for the first few years, until we turned a profit. I have a small amount of savings of my own, but not nearly enough—and Rory was dead set against putting any of our money into the business. Said it would be a conflict of interest, what with the council having the final say in who gets the site lease."

"The idea for the cookery school, this came from you or Mademoiselle Miranda?"

"Oh, it was all Miranda. At least at the start. She said she wanted to do something more hands-on, that she was getting bored of all the TV shows. But, frankly, I don't think the project would have got off the ground without me on board."

Angie spoke without pride, in simple matter-of-fact tones like she was talking about a recipe for chocolate cake. It struck Arthur that here was a woman who knew her worth, and not an ounce more or less.

"I really don't think Miranda realised how much *work* it takes to make something like this happen," she continued. "I used to help out with Rory's furniture business in my spare time, so at least I had some idea of how things should be run. But we were getting there. It was all panning out . . ."

They stared down at the plans and flyers before them; the remains of a business, stillborn.

Angie seemed to wake from her reverie. "Did you say the police left the front door unlocked? I suppose I should have words with them, if so. It's really quite irresponsible of them."

"Ah." Chef Maurice gave a little cough. "I am afraid that we must make a confession to you. It was we—"

"And by 'we', he means *him*, I might add—"

"—who ensured the door would be unlocked after the police went away. We are making, you see, an investigation into the murder of Mademoiselle Miranda."

"You are? Thank goodness!" Angie clasped her hands together.

Arthur and Chef Maurice exchanged a puzzled look. This was not how things usually went.

"I read in the local paper all about how you helped figure out those two horrible murders last winter, and I thought it was all so clever of you."

"Ah, you are too kind, *madame*," said Chef Maurice, standing up a little straighter even so.

"And, well, I didn't really know what I could say to you, to— to—"

"Make us take up the enquiry, perhaps?"

Angie nodded.

"In fact, this is what you wished to speak to us of, the day of the Fayre, *n'est-ce pas*?"

Angie nodded again. "I'll help with whatever I can, of course. And if we find out anything, we'll be sure to tell the police straight away, it won't be like we're going behind their backs. I'm sure they won't mind, really—"

"Hah," muttered Arthur.

"You know," she sighed, "even just saying this, I feel such a whole lot better. Being able to *do* something about it all, instead of just sitting around waiting to hear of any more news."

Chef Maurice placed a hand on Angie's arm. "Come, *madame*, you must tell us more," he said, leading them back into the living room. "If Arthur will make us some tea—"

"Pot wash *and* tea lady," grumbled Arthur.

"—you must tell us all you can of Mademoiselle Miranda. You have been, how do they say, firm friends for a long time?"

"Oh, yes. We were in the same class at Lady Eleanor, from the first year all the way up to Sixth Form. But then we mostly lost touch when I went to do my teacher training down in Bournemouth, and Miranda got sent off to Paris to study at Le Cordon Bleu. We exchanged a few letters at the start, but I hadn't seen her for years until she moved back to these parts."

"When was this?" asked Arthur, from over by the kettle.

"About six months ago. She quite surprised me. I mean, I'd seen her on all her cookery shows, of course, but I never got round to getting in touch properly. I thought she'd be much too busy with all her shows and cookbooks and all."

"Do you know what brought her back to the area?" asked Arthur. "Does she have family nearby?"

Angie shook her head. "It's quite sad, but I don't think she had much family to begin with. She lived with her aunt after her parents died when she was little—a boating accident, I think—then she got sent here to Lady Eleanor. I suppose her aunt thought it was best for her to spend time around other children, instead of living up in the middle of nowhere. I think Miranda just liked this area. She had good memories here, I suppose. She said the Cotswolds were so peaceful, after all her years in London and Paris."

"And Mademoiselle Miranda was happy here in Cowton? She made no mention of any trouble in her life?"

"I've been thinking about that," said Angie, absent-mindedly arranging the coasters on the coffee table.

"She never said anything, but I could tell something was bothering her. I tried asking her about it a few times, but she said I'd be better off not knowing, that she'd tell me once it was all 'sorted'." Angie bit her lip. "If only I'd managed to get it out of her."

"One cannot think too much on the past. Now, I must ask a question of some delicacy," said Chef Maurice, who personally had no qualms in such matters. "Who is it who benefits from the death of Mademoiselle Miranda? You said she has little family, *non*?"

"Yes, just her aunt, as far as I know. I guess Miranda would have left everything to her."

"Ah, that is most interesting," said Chef Maurice, with a significant look in Arthur's direction.

"Oh! But surely you can't be implying her aunt has anything to do with all this?" Angie looked aghast. "She must be well into her eighties by now. And she lives up in the Inner Hebrides. I don't know if the police have even been able to contact her yet. Miranda said she didn't even have a phone line."

"Even so, one must leave no stone upside down." Chef Maurice accepted the brimming cup of tea from Arthur and spooned in three sugars. "You said you came to check that the *appartement* was properly locked. There are, therefore, many items of value in here?"

"Well, there's the furniture, of course. But I was thinking more about Miranda's jewellery. And her photography equipment. She took all those herself, you know," she said, gesturing at the wildlife prints around the walls. "She won an award a few years ago, for her work photographing endangered species. She was always keen on photography, even back when we were in school. Of course, it was all messing around with chemicals and darkrooms in those days."

"Aha, then that is one mystery already solved." Chef Maurice filled them in on PC Alistair's muddy discovery last Saturday. "Perhaps Mademoiselle Miranda took her camera to go photograph the birds and animals of Warren's Creek?"

"I suppose she might have," said Angie, a trifle doubtful.

Arthur tried to picture Miranda Matthews stalking through the English woodlands with her neon nails and cream-coloured jeans. It was a picture that didn't quite fit.

"Bof," said Chef Maurice eventually. "Come, we cannot sit here drinking tea like the English ladies. Let us continue!"

Thus galvanised, they headed through to the master bedroom, which was decorated in tasteful greys and dominated by a king-sized bed, the satin sheets still rumpled. The wardrobes were bulging with assorted designer items, crammed in with no thought to any seasonal or functional arrangement, or so it seemed to Arthur, while a wide chest of drawers was dedicated entirely to high-heeled shoes in a variety of garish colours.

"What exactly are we looking for?" said Angie to Arthur, as Chef Maurice dived in, banging open cupboards and riffling through drawers.

"I suspect we'll know it when we see it," said Arthur,

opening a drawer filled with neatly arranged bras of all colours, and closing it again hastily.

"Aha! *Cherchez l'homme!*" Chef Maurice had zoned in on the bedside table drawer, and now held up a framed black-and-white photo of a good-looking, if somewhat brooding, man in his early forties.

"That's Adam Monroe, Miranda's ex-boyfriend," said Angie. "I never met him. I think they broke up before she moved here."

"Could he have been the cause of her moving here, even?" suggested Arthur.

"I don't know, I didn't ask. He was a rotten sort anyway, from what I heard. It was all over the papers." She gave a little sniff. "Certain papers, anyway. He cheated on her, you know?"

Arthur, who confined his morning reading to the *England Observer* and a few other broadsheets, and Chef Maurice, who preferred to receive his news in accordance with the time-honoured principle that if it was important enough, someone would tell him, both shook their heads.

"Miranda always said that karma got him in the end, though. Two weeks later, he got fired off that soap opera of his. They had his character go bungee-jumping with a faulty cord. And to think he tried to blame it all on Miranda. As if she could have had anything to do with it."

"Him being fired, you mean?"

"Exactly. A spiteful idea on his part."

Arthur looked down at Adam Monroe's square-jawed profile. A ladykiller, for sure, but in how many senses of the word?

"Hmm. We could be looking at a case of a disgruntled ex."

"*C'est possible*," murmured Chef Maurice, still holding the photo. Then, with a sudden 'Aha!', he jumped up and scuttled back out into the kitchen.

"It is *him*. And *her*!" He jabbed a finger at the redhead in the magazine cover shoot. "They were together, at the Fayre. They made a most big distraction in the queue for my hog roast!"

Arthur grabbed the photo from Chef Maurice's waving hand. The chef was right. Slap a pair of dark sunglasses onto the surly lothario in the frame, and add a few decades onto the flame-haired girl, and you had the couple who'd been participating in the extended smoochfest in the hog roast queue.

"By George, you're right. It's definitely them!"

"Adam Monroe was at the Fayre, with *Gaby*?" Angie looked thoroughly confused. "What could he have been doing here? I thought he lived in London. And with her?"

"When exactly did he and Miranda break up?" asked Arthur.

"I don't quite know. I got the impression it was on and off for quite a while, but him being caught with that blonde motoring show presenter was the last straw."

"Could it be just a coincidence? Him being at the

Fayre?" asked Arthur, though rather doubtfully.

"The ex-boyfriend and the ex-*collègue* of Mademoiselle Miranda, together on the day of her murder? *Mon ami*, that is too much. *Non*, there must be a reason . . ."

Angie looked down at her wristwatch and gave a little gasp. "My goodness, how time flies! I'm meant to be having a viewing of the cookery school site right now. It's just down the road from here, and I didn't have the heart to cancel. I suppose part of me wanted to have a look for the last time. It really was the perfect site."

"We will accompany you," said Chef Maurice. "The school was an important plan of Mademoiselle Miranda, and it is important that we learn as much of her as possible."

"I'm sorry we didn't find out much here," said Angie, as she locked up the flat.

"*Non, non*, you must not say that. We only make a beginning. And it will not be over, I promise you, until the fat lady sings a song."

Or, at least until one amply fed head chef got to the bottom of who was responsible for the murder of Miranda Matthews.

Because even if her cooking methods stretched the definition of 'chef' to its outer limits (and then some), she could still be placed on some outlying branch of the great cheffing family tree.

And chefs, as Chef Maurice had declared at the start of that day, should not go around getting murdered.

* * *

Mr Hathaway, of Cowton Country Property Lettings Ltd., was a self-satisfied young man in his thirties, consummate in the ability to deploy such choice phrases as: 'benefiting from extensive renovation', to describe a dilapidated Victorian mid-terrace where the toilet was now actually situated *within* the house; 'brimming with character', in relation to an alleged barn conversion that had yet to rehouse its previous bleating, woolly occupants; and 'ideally located for the London commuter trains', to depict the location of a farmhouse so remote that its inhabitants had developed their own regional dialect.

"Mrs Gifford, what a pleasant surprise," he said, stepping forward to meet them under the faded awning of the now-defunct Cauliflowers and Cupcakes Cookery School. "I wasn't sure if you'd still be coming, what with the dreadful news about poor Miss Matthews. My deepest condolences."

"Thank you," said Angie, as Mr Hathaway clasped her hands awkwardly in his own. It looked like a gesture he'd picked up from a much older man, and completely failed to suit. "I'd like to introduce to you Mr Manchot and Mr Wordington-Smythe, both part of the Beakley Spring Fayre Committee. You don't mind if I show them around the site, do you?"

"Not at all," replied Mr Hathaway, contriving to smile with the corners of his mouth alone. He produced a big bunch of keys, and they stepped inside.

The front room of the shop was set out with rows of worn-looking kitchen worktops, all facing the back of the room, which was a mess of plumbing and electrical wiring.

"That's where we'd set up the demo station," said Angie, waving towards the back wall, "and we'd replace all these benches, of course. There'd be a row of fridges over on the side there, for the pastry classes. And pantry cupboards back here, for the ingredients for the day. Of course, most of the bulk supplies would have to be stored out the back." She looked over to Mr Hathaway, who was standing by the door with the look of a man who'd heard this spiel a dozen times already. "Do you mind if we go through to the other rooms?"

"By all means, take your time. In fact, if it's all right with you, Mrs Gifford, I'll just leave the keys here, and you can drop them back to Sandra in the office when you're done. I'm afraid I have another viewing in ten minutes across town."

He dealt them all a quick nod, exchanged a few parting pleasantries, then he was gone.

The door at the back of the room opened up into a narrow corridor. Off to the left were the remains of an office of sorts, and next door, an old walk-in fridge, suggesting the building had been used as a restaurant at some point in its life.

"It's not much to look at, at the moment," said Angie, "but layout-wise, there's very little structural change that need to be made. All it needs is a lick of paint, and all new equipment, of course. I'm always amazed what a little TLC can do for a place. I finally talked Rory into letting me do over our kitchen at home. We finally pulled out that dreadful old Victorian stove, which was just sitting there, and got rid of the linoleum. Now it feels like I'm walking into someone else's house."

She ran a finger over a piece of peeling paint, which crumbled to the floor. "They really didn't take much care of this place," she murmured to herself.

Yet there was something in the way she looked around them, something in her voice, that Chef Maurice noticed. She did not speak like a woman wandering through the remains of a now-vanquished dream. She spoke, instead, like one still on the edge of dreaming.

"It seems, *madame*, that you have not yet completely given away the hope for this project, *n'est-ce pas?*"

Angie looked momentarily flustered. "Well . . . I mean, it's a silly thought, really, to think about going on with all this without Miranda. But I can't help feeling . . ." She sighed. "We have the best proposal, I'm sure of it. And, I thought, if we somehow win the lease, I could at least get Rory to help me put together a loan application. It never hurts to try, I've always said."

"There are others, then, who also wish to win this site?" asked Chef Maurice. He pulled open the door to a broom cupboard, then stepped aside as a large spider made its dash for freedom.

"Well, it's not exactly public knowledge," said Angie, twisting her fingers, "but these things seem to get around. Our biggest competition is probably Signor Gallo, who owns The Spaghetti Tree next door to here."

"Gallo?" said Arthur. "But what would he be wanting with a cookery school?"

"He apparently wants to knock through from his restaurant and use half the space to enlarge the dining room, and the rest for a much smaller cookery school. He's been quite aggressive about it all, I have to say. I went round to Miranda's once, and he was up there, practically screaming at her. Telling her that the site should clearly go to him and that we should stay out of it."

"Interesting. And we know Gallo was definitely at the Fayre, doing that pasta demonstration of his," said Arthur in low tones to Chef Maurice.

Angie gave him a wide-eyed look. "You're not suggesting that Signor Gallo had anything to do with . . . what happened? I mean, I know what I just said about him and Miranda, but it's just the Latin spirit in him, I'm sure. He's always been so charming when Rory and I go there for dinner."

"Madame Angie, you are too kind in the heart. In the search for a criminal, you must be willing to consider all who you meet," said Chef Maurice, waggling a finger. "And you must not be fooled. Even the worst type of murderer, for example, may be a good man to his own dog."

"Was there anyone else?" said Arthur.

"I only heard about one other application. From Mr Bonvivant."

"Eh?" Chef Maurice stopped in the process of inspecting the shelves in the back storeroom. "Bonvivant? That *imbécile* of a man, who calls himself a chef but spends more time looking in the mirror than at the plates he sends to his guests? What does he require this place for? He has already a cookery school at his restaurant. All made of glass, and with the ovens with too many buttons!"

"Didn't I see you looking at a brochure after that last time we visited him?" said Arthur, which earned him a frosty glare.

"Miranda reckoned he didn't want another cookery school setting up in this area," explained Angie. "He said he was going to run it as an offshoot of his own school, but really, it'd just be to keep everyone else out of the market. There aren't a lot of available sites in central Cowton, and the council's ever so strict on having the right mix of shops and restaurants. Rory seems to spend half his time arguing with shop owners about what they can and can't do with the properties. So if one of the other two gets the lease, there's no chance of opening up another cookery school nearby." She gave a sad little sigh.

"And Bonvivant, did he too make threats to Mademoiselle Miranda?"

"I didn't hear about any," replied Angie, to Chef Maurice's disappointment.

"Ah, still, we cannot leave him from our investigation. It is in his interest that you and Mademoiselle Miranda did not continue this project." He stooped down to retrieve a long-trampled flyer from the ground.

Cauliflowers and Cupcakes presents the Competent Chef Cookery Course! Cook like a pro in only ten weeks! Every Monday, 7-9pm.

"Bah! Ten weeks? Three months, it was, before Alf could make *un bon mousse au chocolat*! How dare they make these claims? It is no wonder that they closed!"

"I heard it was because the last owners won the lottery and moved to Barbados," said Arthur.

"Humph!"

"You really think that the murder might have something to do with the cookery school?" said Angie, as they wandered back out through the main classroom.

"One must consider all the boulevards," was Chef Maurice's gnomic reply.

Angie left Arthur and Chef Maurice outside on the pavement, to run over to return the keys before she drove over to the Lady Eleanor School to teach her afternoon classes. She promised to quiz her mayoral husband later on the subject of any other competitors to her and Miranda in the bid for the cookery school site.

"And we've still got that suspicious appearance by Miranda's ex-boyfriend to look into," said Arthur, flipping through the notes he'd made at Miranda's flat. "So what's the plan now?"

Chef Maurice jabbed a thumb at the sign hanging above them, which depicted a green cartoon tree, its branches draped with spaghetti.

"We start with the suspect we find the nearest," he said. "And also, it is now time for lunch. The solving of crime, it creates a big appetite, do you not think?"

CHAPTER 7

Like that of many Italian restaurants of a certain age, The Spaghetti Tree's decor was firmly mired in the Eighties, complete with plastic red-and-white-check tablecloths, rickety wooden chairs, and faded photos in black frames showing Signor Gallo pressing the flesh with various celebrities and dignitaries who, from the uncertain grins on their faces, most likely had no idea what they were doing in Cowton and would be hard-pressed now to locate the town, even with the help of a large-scale road map helpfully opened to 'C'.

"Look, I know you're keen to speak to Gallo about this whole cookery school business," said Arthur, from somewhere behind a tall and somewhat sticky laminated menu, "but did we really have to eat here too? I'm not exactly the staff's favourite person at the moment."

"Ah, *oui*? The Spaghetti Tree did not survive well under your pen?"

The life of a restaurant critic was one spent doling out various measures of praise and censure—often in unequal amounts, as there was nothing the readers of the *England Observer* liked better than the good and thorough roasting of a highfalutin restaurant that had got a little too big for its boots and required Arthur's rapier pen to deliver some much needed ego-deflation.

This also had the result of Arthur becoming a *persona non grata* in many dining rooms up and down the country, but this was not something that often caused him any bother, up until now.

"Hmm. I do recall comparing their mozzarella to eating a white bathing cap filled with old skimmed milk . . ."

"Ah. And?" Arthur's reviews never went easy once he had descended for the kill.

"And I might have made some comment about the home-made meatballs tasting like something you'd find in a service station microwave meal."

"Yet everyone says that the recipe was given to him by his dear old *nonna*."

Arthur snorted. "Unlikely, for a man who was born Bob Higgins, and only changed his name to Roberto Gallo when he opened up this place. And that fake accent of his, it borders on the ridiculous!"

Chef Maurice had to agree, though personally he had always been rather impressed by the restaurateur's dedication to his hastily adopted new culture. The man knew no half measures; every time he announced his *pasta arrabiata*, diners would wince and hide behind their menus to avoid the extraneous spittle.

"Still, *mon ami*, it is important that we speak with Monsieur Gallo. And it is not right to run in here shouting our questions. We must make an approach *diplomatique*."

Their discussion was halted by a compact but well-rounded stomach floating into view at the side of the table. It was attached to Signor Gallo himself, dressed, as usual, like a down-on-his-luck opera singer.

"Welcome, *signori*, to The Spaghetti—" He stopped as he looked down and noticed Arthur for the first time. His mouth opened and closed soundlessly, while his face tried on a range of hues, from beetroot purple to white with hints of rage, until settling for an alarming shade of maroon.

"*Bonjour*, Monsieur Gallo," said Chef Maurice. "You have met my friend, Monsieur Wordington-Smythe?"

Signor Gallo had now managed to force his features into a rictus of a smile. "Signor Wordington-Smythe, how kind of you to choose to dine with us *again*. I will be sure to let our head chef know."

No mafia boss pronouncement could have sounded quite as chilling as that last particular statement.

"Oh, er, capital. Maurice, were you ready to order?"

Chef Maurice nodded, selecting the bruschetta with tomatoes and olive tapenade, followed by a mushroom-and-taleggio-cheese polenta, and put in a reservation for a portion of the allegedly 'home-made' tiramisu.

Arthur, with a fearful glance towards the kitchens, declared himself to be oddly full still from breakfast, and ordered a double espresso.

"You are sure, *signor*, that you are not hungry?" said Signor Gallo with a leer, as Arthur's stomach gave a traitorous little rumble.

"Not at all, I assure you. Another time, perhaps."

"Verrrry well. Then you will not be needing these." With an oily smile, Signor Gallo snatched the breadsticks off the table and traipsed away towards the kitchen.

"Tch, now you have lost us our pre-starter," grumbled Chef Maurice, who was partial to bread in any form.

"They taste like compressed sawdust, believe me."

Thankfully for the nearby tables, whose main courses were now being subjected to some longing stares, Chef Maurice's starter turned up not long after. Arthur stared at it in amazement.

The tomato was expertly diced into bright red little jewels, a far cry from the usual anaemic-looking specimens found in the British supermarkets. The tapenade glistened, the bread was toasted golden, and the whole dish was garnished with torn basil and what smelt like freshly pressed olive oil.

"You are sure you do not wish to order?" said Chef Maurice, tucking into his dish with gusto. "The ingredients, they are most pleasingly fresh."

"He's doing this on purpose." Arthur threw a dark look at Signor Gallo, who was now charming a table of lunching ladies with tales from his ersatz Italian childhood. "I had that same dish when I came. It was nothing like that. He must have a secret stash of olive oil hidden out the back . . ."

Chef Maurice shrugged, and ordered a large glass of chilled Vermentino to accompany his meal.

Signor Gallo soon returned with the main dish, a generous portion of polenta, with the scent of tangy taleggio wafting up from the warmed plate.

"I thought Signor Wordington-Smythe might be now feeling hungry, so I asked my head chef to prepare him a special dish." A silver-domed platter was placed before Arthur.

The dome was whisked away, to reveal a bulging white bathing cap.

"Hilarious," muttered Arthur, while his stomach gave another little growl.

It was halfway through the superlative tiramisu—"I'll bet you anything they popped out and bought it from the patisserie across the road"—when Chef Maurice decided it was time to broach the topic of Miranda Matthews with their good host, who was fussing around nearby, placing new baskets of breadsticks on all the tables around them.

"Is what I hear true, Monsieur Gallo, that you plan to open a cookery school in the shop next to here?"

"*Sì!* It has been an idea of mine and Maria's for a long time. We will enlarge our space, and Maria will teach pasta-making classes for the children." He waved a hand at Maria, née Mary, who ran the front of house and, unlike her husband, had been unwilling to surrender her native Yorkshire accent.

"But there is some competition, I understand, for the site?"

Signor Gallo gave him a suspicious look. "Where did you hear that?"

"We were speaking earlier to Madame Angie—"

"Ah, the mayor's wife? *Sì*. I told Maria, the council should not have let that woman apply! A clear case of conflicting interests. But never mind," he added, with a shrug, "without her business partner, she cannot continue now. I hear she has no money of her own."

"Ah, *oui*? But Madame Angie has given hint that this may no longer be the case," said Chef Maurice, who generally liked to stir things up.

But Signor Gallo would not be drawn. "Whatever the case, if that woman wins, I will make my protests to the council. Did you know, they made attempts to make me withdraw my case by threatening and harassing me?"

"Angie Gifford?" said Arthur. "Harassing you? I can hardly believe that."

Chef Maurice agreed. It was easier to imagine a duckling, perhaps one in the throes of an identity crisis, taking down a fully grown swan than to picture Angela Gifford even mildly taking anyone to task.

"Ah, no, not that one. But the tall one, with the ridiculous big hair. Everywhere I go, she follows me! I take Maria out for dinner, and she is there. I go for my Pilates class, and she is there!" Signor Gallo ran a hand through his greasy black hair. "I thought at first she was trying to seduce me—"

Chef Maurice choked on a mouthful of tiramisu.

"—and so I tell her, *signorina*, I am sorry but I am a one-woman man. And yet, she continues. Sometimes she tries to hide away, but I still see her!"

"Did you contact the police, then?" asked Arthur.

Signor Gallo looked uncomfortable. "I did not wish to make a fuss. And now, there is no need. She brought her fate down onto her, with her wickedness," he added, with some satisfaction.

"You were at the Fayre, perhaps," said Chef Maurice, "when the finding of the body was made? I do not remember seeing you at that time."

"No, I had returned here after my pasta-making demonstration to open up the restaurant. Maria, she stayed at the Fayre. She tells me two married women were taken by the police for questioning. The wives whose husbands were entrapped by the dangerous *signorina*, I am sure, and who therefore took their revenge."

Satisfied with his solution to the crime, Signor Gallo left them to join in a rousing chorus of '*buon compleanno!*', directed at a timid five-year-old wearing a party hat and a fearful expression.

"So what do you make of that?" said Arthur, leaning over the table. "Do you believe his alibi, about coming back here after his demo?"

"Hmm, it will be difficult to check. His staff, they will make lies for him, of course."

"What about the customers?"

"Ah, that is true. We will ask questions around. But remember, his wife, Maria, she was also at the Fayre, and could have been the one to commit the crime. And he was fast to admit that without Madame Angie and Mademoiselle Miranda in the run, they have now a much greater chance to gain the cookery school site."

"As does Bonvivant, don't forget. Though I have to say, clobbering someone over the head with a drainpipe doesn't really seem to fit his style."

"*Oui*, that is true." If Gustave Bonvivant was going to murder someone, one would expect it to involve a lot of well-tailored black and stiletto knives in the dark.

But still, there was no harm in making some gentle enquiries . . .

They paid the bill and headed for Chef Maurice's car, stopping along the way for Arthur to pick up a jumbo sausage roll and a cream bun from the local bakery.

"If Meryl asks, you did not see me eat this," he said, waving the bun.

Thus provisioned, they motored out into the Oxfordshire countryside, windows down, leaving a trail of flaky pastry in their wake.

As one of the county's few fine dining establishments of note, L'Epicure boasted a reservations diary that filled up several months in advance, leaving the area's more unorganised husbands in a panicked flurry every time Valentine's Day and various anniversaries came unexpectedly around. It was easier, they complained, to become Prime Minister than it was to get a Saturday evening table at short notice at Chef Bonvivant's restaurant.

However, as impenetrable as the dining room of L'Epicure might have been, when it came to gaining access to its kitchens, this was a simple matter of walking around the back of the building until one came across a likely-looking set of swinging doors. The handful of lanky chefs and off-duty waiters hanging around, puffing on dog-eared cigarettes, was also a handy giveaway.

Chef Maurice and Arthur received a few questioning glances as they ambled through the sprawling kitchens, but all of Bonvivant's chefs and waitstaff had been trained to recognise the country's key food critics—in fact, their pictures, cut out from various magazines, were enlarged and tacked above the main door leading to the dining rooms—and so assumed that if the restaurant critic from the *England Observer* was wandering around in their midst, then he was clearly meant to be there and it would be best not to disturb him. In fact, he was probably being shown around by that PR chap with the huge moustache.

Also, the majority of the kitchen crew were currently oblivious to their surroundings, completely engrossed as they were with their peas.

They all stood around a large shiny prep station, heads bowed over two stainless steel bowls each, one containing a big heap of dried black-eyed peas. The Herculean task at hand appeared to be to move the pile of peas from one bowl to the other, using a set of very long, very pointy chopsticks.

There were various *pings* as escaping peas popped from tense chopstick grips, accompanied by the kind of heated swearing usually associated with the worst type of sailors.

"Maurice, Arthur! What a pleasant surprise to see you here. You have come to view my new training program?"

Chef Bonvivant, spotless as always in chef's whites and a tall white toque, appeared through the swinging dining room doors, trailed by his ever-present assistant.

"Looks like you've quite revolutionised the transport of dried peas," commented Arthur.

"Ha ha. No, not exactly. I spent the whole of last month in Japan, visiting the kitchens of some of their most prestigious establishments. Did you know, some of them don't even allow reservations from the public—to eat there, one must be introduced by another diner. If only one might introduce such a concept in this country," he added with a sigh, perhaps at the thought of his own woefully mixed bag of clientele.

"And the dishes they create," he continued, "I have never seen such exquisiteness. And everything done with chopsticks! So much more delicate, finessed, when you plate a dish without the need for these." He wiggled his own elegantly tapered fingers.

"So how do you find the using of the chopsticks, *jeune homme*?" said Chef Maurice to a young man with a ginger crew cut who was bent over his bowl, his tongue poked out in ferocious concentration.

The young chef hesitated, with a quick look over at Chef Bonvivant's face. "Not as fast as I'd like to be, sir, but I'm practicing lots."

"I keep finding peas all over my station," complained a voice down the end of the bench.

"Plus it's slower than watching a sloth take a sh—" began yet another, before Chef Bonvivant hurriedly cut in.

"Yes, we're still in the adoption phase, of course, but I am certain we will get there with the necessary application and mindset," he said, glaring at the third chef. "So do I take it that you have come to visit to watch my staff count beans? Or perhaps you are looking for a new sous-chef." He gave Chef Maurice a brief, sharklike smile.

"You are wrong in both ways. We come to speak to you about Mademoiselle Miranda Matthews," said Chef Maurice, making a mental note to berate Dorothy for her gossipy tendencies.

"Oh? Don't tell me, Maurice, that you're getting yourself involved in yet another murder investigation? Too much time out from the kitchen will surely be bad for your staff's morale."

"I heard Patrick say they get more done without him, actually," chipped in Arthur.

"Hah, the mutterings of a traitor," said Chef Maurice darkly. He turned back to Chef Bonvivant. "You were there at the Fayre, *n'est-ce pas*, when the attack happened?"

"Yes, but I'm afraid I don't see what that has to do with anything."

"Mademoiselle Miranda and Madame Gifford were intending to open a cookery school. A site which, I hear, you are most interested in, too."

"My team have put in a bid for the Cowton site, yes," said Chef Bonvivant, leaning over and using a pair of chopsticks to pick up the peas that had escaped across the table, in a series of deft little movements. All around him, the pea-transportation efforts doubled at this sight.

"Ah, so you admit that the murder of Mademoiselle Miranda has been of benefit to you and your business."

"I do not think so. I do not expect that the council would have granted those two the lease, no matter the circumstance. A TV chef and a school teacher? Much better to place the site in experienced hands such as ours. Anyway, from my point of view, the whole ordeal has probably been more trouble than it's worth."

"Ah, *oui?*"

"It might amuse you to know that, far from me having anything to do with that dreadful woman, it was *her* who came poking around here. I found her sneaking about in my kitchens a few weeks ago, using her feminine wiles on my staff." He narrowed his eyes at the group around the table and a dozen young men blushed furiously. "I asked her what she was doing here, and she said she came to warn me. She dared to suggest something 'unfortunate' might happen if I did not drop the application. I told her I was sure she was used to getting her own way in the world of television cookery"—a sneer was here inserted—"but that the real world did not work quite like that. She left here in quite a temper."

"*Oui*, she did not seem a woman very *charmante*, Mademoiselle Miranda."

"In truth, I cannot claim enthusiasm at the thought of running two cookery school sites. It will necessitate the transfer of some of our teaching staff. But we have also been making enquiries into opening a bistro along the Cowton High Street too, so perhaps the two will be able to work in conjunction."

"You're branching out into Cowton?" said Arthur. "It's a competitive market, I hear."

"But lacking in French dining options, I believe. And given how well Maurice's little place does, one suspects there is definitely room in the market for some growth."

They took their leave soon after, at Arthur's insistence, before Chef Maurice could do any damage to Chef Bonvivant with a well-placed pair of chopsticks.

"That man, he is *intolérable*," fumed the chef, as they strolled back to the car through the restaurant's carefully tended vegetable gardens. ("Humph, it is all for show," he added. "He buys from the same vegetable producers as I do, I have seen his invoices.")

"But, unfortunately, in possession of a rather good alibi. I had a quick word with one of his commis. He was at the scallop stand the whole of lunchtime on Saturday. No breaks."

"Bah, then he instructed one of his kitchen staff—"

"What, to carry out murder? I don't think employer loyalty stretches quite that far, at least not these days."

"Humph. Very true. The loyalty, today, it is all gone," said Chef Maurice, bristling at the thought of his so-easily-swayed sous-chef.

"Oh, come now, the chap's got a hard choice to make. You can't go making his decisions for him, you know."

"Why is it that everyone tells me that?" grumbled Chef Maurice.

He reached into a pocket and pulled out his wristwatch. He was fairly certain that by now Patrick would have insisted on returning the ThermoMash. It was exactly the type of high-minded thing his sous-chef would do.

That said, Chef Maurice would not be entirely unhappy to see the restaurant's bank balance return to a much more healthy figure. Especially with the annual Paris Cheese Fair just around the corner, which always made a serious dent in the yearly finances.

Just then, Arthur's phone buzzed. It was Zara Brightwell, one of Meryl's friends who ran a clothing boutique on the Cowton High Street, opposite The Spaghetti Tree.

"Hi Zara, you got my message? . . . Uh-huh . . . Uh-huh." Arthur listened for a while longer, then hung up with assurances that he and Meryl would be delighted to come over to theirs for dinner next Saturday.

"She's a terrible cook, but what can one do," he said, tucking the phone away. "Anyway, it seems that Gallo did go back to his restaurant before lunchtime last Saturday, just like he said. And Maria apparently has had frozen shoulder for the last few years—can't lift a tea tray, let alone a big piece of piping. That rather puts paid to this whole cookery school angle. So what's our next move, old chap?"

"Hmm. You say we are finished with the idea of the cookery school, but it is possible that Madame Angie is mistaken. There may be others that still make a bid for the site."

"Possible. But how do you propose we find them?"

"Simple, *mon ami*. We go, as they say, to the donkey's mouth."

"I think you mean horse, Maurice."

"Ah, *oui*? That is interesting. One would think that a donkey is the one who talks the most."

Mr Paul Whittaker, Deputy Mayor of Cowton, had the sort of face and bearing that called to mind a Thoroughbred racehorse. Arthur, who had met the man previously at a few official dinners, had described him as rather aquiline in feature, but Chef Maurice disagreed—there was nothing watery or wishy-washy, he argued, about the deputy mayor in the slightest. If anything, Paul Whittaker had a type of parchedness to his personality, and certainly his hands were dry as sandpaper as he shook their own and settled them into the two chairs across from his desk.

His was a small, narrow office, though fitted out with all the accoutrements of a much larger room. The walls were adorned with various black-and-white photographs of vintage sports cars, and above his desk hung an oil painting of a severe-looking gentleman with a distinctly horsey expression.

"My father," said Mr Whittaker, noticing their glances. "He held office as Mayor of Cowton for eighteen years. And his father before him." He nodded at the portrait on the far wall (which, given the size of the room, was not very far at all). "He himself held office for twenty-five years, the longest term held by any mayor in Cowton's history."

"How long has Mayor Gifford's term been so far?" said Arthur.

"I believe it will be fifteen years this summer. But, sadly for us, it appears that national politics will be taking him away from the Town Hall, if the local elections go as expected. My apologies that he couldn't see you today, by the way. He's attending a farming conference in Cheltenham." Mr Whittaker squared the pad of paper before him. "You said you had an urgent matter to discuss with him. Hopefully I can be of assistance instead?"

"*Oui*, we hope," said Chef Maurice. "It concerns the cookery school site on the High Street."

"Oh, yes. The site next to The Spaghetti Tree. But I'm afraid that applications are now closed."

"Ah, but I do not wish to apply for the site."

"Oh?"

"I simply wish to make enquiries as to the other applicants. It is a matter of much urgency, you see."

112

"I see." Mr Whittaker made a small note on his pad, reminding himself to have a few words with the receptionist about what constituted an urgent request for mayoral (or at least, deputy-mayoral) attention. "I'm afraid applications are of course a confidential matter, as you—"

"One of your applicants has been the victim of murder! Now, *monsieur*, is not the time for the blue tape." He gave Mr Whittaker a stern look. "The office of the mayor, it is to serve the citizens of Cowton, is it not? And yet, here you sit, with one of them murdered, and you refuse to lend your aid? The people, they will not be happy," he added, with the gravity of a man hailing from a country where a lot of unhappy people had, eventually, led to the fame of one Monsieur Guillotin.

Mr Whittaker made a quick mental calculation regarding the reasonably attainable speed of ejection of his unwanted visitors versus the probability of getting into trouble for the disclosure of confidential information. "Well, as the list of applicants will technically be available on request, once the decision is formally announced later this week, I suppose there is no harm in revealing it at this point. As long as such information is not disseminated any further, you understand."

"You have my word, *monsieur*."

Mr Whittaker cleared his throat. "As you already seem to be aware, Miranda Matthews, along with her business partner Angela Gifford, was one of the applicants—"

"And a strong applicant too, *n'est-ce pas?*"

113

Mr Whittaker adjusted his face to resemble a lake with a large 'No Fishing' sign. "All the applications had their various merits, of course. Miranda Matthews provided the strongest marketing proposal, but this is not surprising given her media background. As a supporter of local business, there are, however, many other factors we must consider when deciding upon a new let. Now, as for the other two—"

"*Oui*, Monsieur Gallo of The Spaghetti Tree and Monsieur Bonvivant of L'Epicure. These we already know of. But there were no others?"

"Sorry? No, those are the whole list. In fact, we were fairly surprised there were that many, to tell the truth." Mr Whittaker frowned. "I don't quite see, given how you seem to be quite well-informed in these matters, why—"

But Chef Maurice was already standing up, replacing his pork-pie hat on his head. "*Merci beaucoup*, Monsieur Whittaker, we will not take away any more of your time. You have been most helpful. Come, Arthur, let us continue, now that we have closed this angle, *non?*"

They left Mr Whittaker sitting alone in his small office, with only the portraits of Mr Whittaker (Snr.) and Mr Whittaker (V. Snr.) for company.

After a few moments spent staring down at his notepad, in apparent deep contemplation, the deputy mayor roused himself and pressed the buzzer on his desk.

"Gemma," he said, crisply, "we need to have a discussion as to the definition of an 'urgent matter'. Sorry, what? No, I do not want a cream bun. Thank you."

* * *

"Bingo!" said PC Sara, putting down the phone.

PC Lucy looked up from her current task of trawling the Internet for all things Miranda Matthews-related. She'd only been at it for half an hour, but had already hauled in a bountiful catch. Thank goodness for the online gossip rags, was all she could say. "What've you found?"

"They've managed to trace the missed call Miranda received on the day of the Fayre. Any guesses whose number it is?"

"I thought we agreed on a ban on guessing games."

"Fine. It was Adam Monroe, Miranda's ex-boyfriend."

"Now, that *is* interesting."

Chef Maurice and Arthur had stopped round earlier to report the sighting of the same Adam Monroe, spotted 'canoodling' with Miranda's ex-co-host, Gaby Florence, at last Saturday's Fayre.

They had also deigned to inform her that Signor Gallo and Chef Bonvivant were, in their view, currently free from any suspicion—at least when it came to the murder of Miranda Matthews.

PC Lucy, ushering them back out of the office, did not bother asking them what their initial suspicions had been. She also informed Arthur that if a restaurant wished to source its tiramisu from the patisserie across the road, it was entirely its own affair and not a concern for the Cowton and Beakley Constabulary.

"Right, I think it's time we give this Adam Monroe a call." PC Lucy reached over her desk to grab the handset, while PC Sara scooched her chair over and hit the 'speakerphone' button.

"Hello?" said the sleepy male voice on the other end of the line. PC Lucy glanced up at the clock. It was well past three in the afternoon, and she took an instant dislike to the man.

"Good afternoon. This is PC Gavistone of the Cowton and Beakley Constabulary in Oxfordshire. May I please speak with Mr Adam Monroe?"

There was a pause. "How'd you get this number?" He sounded definitely more awake now.

"Mr Monroe, I'm sure you're aware of the unfortunate death of Miranda Matthews this w—"

"Of course I'm bloody aware! Everybody's been ringing me up non-stop since the weekend to tell me all about it! And it's not like we've been a couple since, well, back sometime last year now. We didn't bother keeping in touch, I can't think why people think I give a monkey's—"

"If you didn't keep in touch, do you mind me asking why our records show you tried contacting Miranda on her mobile at nine fifty-two last Saturday morning?"

Another pause.

"She didn't pick up. I suppose you know that too, right?" he said, a tad snarkily. "So I gave Miranda a call. So what?"

"Mr Monroe, we have photographic evidence showing that you were at the Beakley Spring Fayre this Saturday. With Gaby Florence, who I understand was also an acquaintance of Miss Matthews'?"

After Chef Maurice and Arthur had left, PC Lucy had taken a quick look back through the photos from the Fayre. Sure enough, the couple showed up in the background of several shots, easily picked out by Adam Monroe's dark glasses and Gaby Florence's fiery locks. It galled her that it had taken a French chef and a food critic to bring this to her attention, but Adam Monroe didn't have to know that.

"Look," said Adam, a tinge of worry creeping into his voice, "I'll be straight with you, okay? I had no idea Miranda was even going to be there, till I saw one of those Bake Off posters on the drive over. It was all Gaby's idea. I swear."

"And Gaby's idea was to do what exactly?"

"What? For us to be there, together. In front of Miranda. Gaby thought it'd be funny. After all these years, beats me why she still has it in for her. I mean, look at me. Miranda cost me my best-paying job in a long while, but you don't see me griping on about it, do you?"

Perhaps, thought PC Lucy, because he had soon after been picked up for a part in the award-winning period drama *du moment*, which was making waves on both sides of the Atlantic. PC Sara was a secret fan, and had been expounding lately on the hitherto overlooked attractiveness of men with bushy sideburns.

"So, when we stopped to get petrol and Gaby went off into the shops, I thought I'd call Miranda, just give her a heads-up that we'd be there."

"That was rather considerate of you."

"Well, I like to keep a low profile. No sense stirring things up."

Or, more likely, his new producers were keen for their cast to stay out of the headlines, unless for the right reasons. And helping to start a celebrity catfight at a country fair probably didn't count as one of those.

"A long way for you both to travel, wasn't it? Just for a village fair."

"Not really. My folks have a holiday cottage out near Chipping Norton. And like I said, it was all Gaby's idea. She said she wanted to go to one of those fairs like the ones she went to as a kid. I mean, once I saw the posters, I twigged that all she wanted was to parade me around in front of Miranda, like a show pony. Women, eh?"

"You're suggesting she wanted to make Miranda jealous? I thought Miranda was the one who ended the relationship," said PC Lucy, brow furrowed as she clicked quickly through the tabloid articles on screen.

"Goodness me, you can't go believing everything you read in the papers, my dear," said Adam, slipping into the country squire accent he used on air. But at least he seemed to be warming to the conversation. "No, I was the one who ended it. Wasn't worth all the aggro in the end. A right crazy bitch, she was, ringing me up all the time, asking where I was. I found out later she'd even paid my building's concierge to phone her up every time I went out the door. Paranoid, if you ask me."

"Even given your somewhat chequered love life, Mr Monroe?"

Adam seemed amused by this. "Done your research, haven't you? Look, I'm not saying I've always been a saint, but this time, I wasn't up to anything. Didn't have the time, for one. But she wasn't having any of it. Almost made me want to go out and prove her right, you know what I mean? When a woman's always on your case, asking why you took twenty minutes instead of ten to get from Bond Street to Soho, I mean, it makes you want to mess around, just for the hell of it. At least you'd be getting something back for all that hassle."

Charming, isn't he? mouthed PC Sara.

"Anyway, yeah, so it was me who ended things. That pushed Miranda right off the deep end. She went total bunny-boiler, if you ask me. Found out I'd started seeing someone new, and so she pulled a whole load of strings with her press chums, and suddenly they're dragging up some stupid quotes of stuff I've said in the past, you know, the kind of thing you say when you're completely rat-arsed and the press are all up in your face. Doesn't mean a thing."

"But it cost you your job, I hear."

"Yeah. My bad luck that I made some joke about some stupid autism charity they were making me go visit, can't even remember what I said now. Anyway, turns out the producer has a daughter with Asperger's. He went all high and mighty on me, and that was it. Out of the job, after eight years being bad boy Derek Peterson."

"Mr Monroe, you're not exactly painting me a picture of someone who had no hard feelings towards Miranda Matthews."

"Nah, like I said, water under the bridge and all that. I take these things easy. Not like Gaby. Now *there's* a bird who can hold a grudge. She's got a chip on her shoulder the size of Iceland about Miranda."

"Oh?" PC Lucy scribbled this down on her notepad. "Rather forthcoming of you, talking about your new girlfriend like that?"

Adam laughed. "Oh, she's not my girlfriend anymore. Dumped me yesterday evening, for talking about Miranda too much. I mean, the woman was murdered! What else was I expected to do, what with everyone ringing me up about it?"

"Tell me more about Gaby and Miranda. Bit of a grudge there, I take it?"

"You could say that. Surely you know the story? No?" Adam sounded surprised. "Everyone knows Gaby's had it in for Miranda ever since the whole 'Wok This Way' debacle."

"That was Miranda's first solo show, right? The one she got chosen for, over Gaby?" PC Lucy was determined to show she'd done at least a modicum of research.

"Chosen?" Adam snorted. "More like Gaby got booted off it, before they even started filming. It was meant to be another double act, this time all about Eastern cuisine, but then Gaby got caught snorting a line of cocaine, and that was that."

"Cocaine?"

"Seriously, you don't know any of this stuff?"

"Feel free to fill in the gaps."

"Okay, so it was like this," said Adam, patently enjoying his role as police gossip informant. "Endline Productions were making the show for the BBC, a prime-time slot, meant to be family-friendly and all that jazz. So Gaby doing a line of coke off a toilet seat in the back of the Horizon Club wasn't exactly the kind of coverage they were aiming for. Rough on her, really, that she got caught. Wasn't as if everyone else wasn't doing exactly the same."

"And she blamed Miranda?"

"The way I heard it, Gaby's always been convinced it was Miranda who leaked those pictures to the press. After all, she'd been there too, that night. Could have easily sneaked some paparazzi fellow in, everyone would have been too off their faces to notice."

"Did Gaby ever manage to prove that Miranda was involved?"

"Nah. Anyway, the photos never made it to print. Gaby paid them off, I heard. But the producers got a whiff of it and that was enough to boot her off the show. And then Miranda went on to make her millions. Nice little story, isn't it?"

"Perhaps. Do you have Miss Florence's contact details?"

"Sure." He reeled off a telephone number and address. "Only you won't get hold of her now. She's on a plane to India. Sent me a message last night, saying she was off to some ashram to cleanse her aura, whatever the hell that means."

"Did she say when she'd be back?"

"Don't know, don't care. And look here," Adam added, now slightly uneasy, "it's not like me and Gaby have any big history or anything. We only hooked up at a mate's birthday bash about a month ago. She was dead keen, guess I now know why. It was all her trying to get one up on Miranda. But hey, I wasn't complaining."

PC Lucy and PC Sara exchanged another 'men, animals the lot of them' look.

"One last question, Mr Monroe. Where were you and Gaby on Saturday afternoon, between the hours of twelve thirty and one fifteen?"

"Ah, so we come to the prime moment. Afraid I'm going to have to disappoint you there. We went to get some lunch, then I spent the rest of the time at the shoot 'em up stand. I had some shooting lessons once, and Gaby wouldn't let me leave until I got her one of those damn stuffed bears. I told her it was ridiculous. Those guns they give you are practically falling to pieces. But then I got a bit caught up in it all, and ended up staying there until I won the biggest one they had. You can talk to the guy at the stall, he'll remember me, all right. Cost me a bloody fortune."

"We will. And what about Miss Florence? Was she with you the whole time?"

"Indeedy. Oh, wait, no, I tell a lie. She took off for the loos at one point. Came back complaining about the queues."

"She was gone a while, then?"

"Yeah. But, I mean, don't quote me on that. It might have been a while, might not have. Couldn't think of anything apart from those damn pink bears, right then."

The conversation ended there, with Adam promising to let them know if he heard again from Gaby.

"Fancy a trip to India?" said PC Sara.

"Doubt the chief will sign that one off. Still, we might as well chase up where Gaby went, see if we can get her on the telephone."

"Not if she's taken one of those vows of silence or something."

"Unlikely. I read she's a radio presenter nowadays. They're not really the silent type."

"That Adam Monroe was pretty full of himself, wasn't he?" said PC Sara, spinning her chair back around to her desk. "Pity. I like a man who looks good in breeches. It's slim pickings in the dating world at the moment. You should be glad you've nabbed that chef fellow of yours."

"We'll see about that." The mention of Patrick gave PC Lucy a dull little ache in her chest. What if he ended up taking the job up in the Lake District? She'd seen enough friends' relationships fizzle out when one of them moved away, usually for job reasons. Of course, they'd always swear that they'd make it work, but eventually the back-and-forth travel and the long-distance phone calls would get too much.

But what could she say? 'It's your mother or me?' The last thing she wanted was to end up in the same crazy camp as Chef Maurice. Patrick had already called her up to rant about the emotional trauma of having to return a state-of-the-art Thermal Masher, or whatever it was.

No, she'd just have to suck it up and play the supportive girlfriend, no matter what his choice.

It didn't stop her, though, wondering idly about what Chef Maurice's next plan of attack would be. And hoping, rather guiltily, that it might just have the desired effect . . .

CHAPTER 8

The next morning, Patrick arrived at the restaurant to find Chef Maurice and Alf hard at work in the dining room, heads bent over a notepad of scribblings.

Given that neither head chef nor commis could possibly be described as naturally early risers—if Chef Maurice was to be found in the kitchens before the hour of six a.m., it could be relied upon that he had not gone to bed the night before—Patrick regarded this impromptu morning tête-à-tête with all due suspicion.

"What's going on?"

"Ah, Patrick! Come, sit." Chef Maurice kicked out the chair opposite him. "The weather, I find it so good, that I have decided we will start our Spring Menu one week early. And I have decided that I must be more, how do you say, loose with my decisions. It is time to let others make a show of their creativity."

"Right."

Clearly, this was yet another move in the sous-chef retention game. Chef Maurice knew how much it rankled him, Patrick, to have to argue, plead and cajole to get each of his new dishes onto Le Cochon Rouge's daily menu. This, though, was definitely a case of too little and much too late.

On the other hand, though, he still had a few days to make his decision, and he had a spice-crusted rainbow trout dish he'd been angling to get onto the—

"And so," continued Chef Maurice, "for our new Spring Menu, I have decided that we will have six new dishes. Two *entrées*, two *plats principaux*, and two desserts. All to be designed by Alf."

A meaty slap was dealt to the gangly commis chef's back. Alf, for his part, looked as if he'd died and gone to a hot, dark place containing a lot of pitchforks.

"Whu-uh?" he managed, not daring to meet Patrick's gaze.

"*Oui!* I have much belief that the best of ideas may come from the places most unexpected. You will present to me your dishes in two days. Now, *allons-y*, there is much preparation to do this morning."

Chef Maurice drained his coffee cup and marched off into the kitchens.

"He's doing this to punish me, isn't he?" said Alf, head in hands.

"Why do you say that?"

"Remember that coriander-flavoured ice cream I made last week by mistake? Instead of using the mint?"

"At least we didn't serve it. And chef managed to offload the whole tub to Arthur in the end. He said he was going to

126

serve it with his cumin chicken at the next dinner party."

"Yeah, but *six* new dishes? Chef knows it's going to be a total disaster. And then I'm going to get the sack."

"He can't do that. He'd have no staff left," said Patrick absently, staring down at Alf's scribblings.

Alf gave a gasp of horror. "Wait, you mean you're actually thinking of *going*?"

Patrick paused. Up until this point, he'd had a firm fence-shaped groove developing under his metaphorical buttocks. But if Chef Maurice was going to continue playing games, then he was damned if he was going to stand around waiting to be hit by a leather ball.

It just wasn't cricket.

"I'm still mulling things over. But I think I'm starting to come to a decision."

Alf, always inclined to baseless optimism, decided to take this as a good sign. "You know, I did have this one idea for a steak dish with glacé cherries and cottage cheese . . ."

Patrick felt immediately queasy as he mentally sampled Alf's proposed dish. And yet . . .

"It's not a bad idea," he found himself saying.

"You think?" Alf looked surprised but gratified.

"It might need a bit of a sauce to go with it. Maybe something like a . . . chocolate-and-grapefruit-infused gravy. Very modern. I can give you a hand with it. Chef will never have to know."

After all, he thought, as Alf scribbled down this stomach-curdling combination, if Chef Maurice was going to stoop to such measures of psycho-culinary warfare, there was no reason why two couldn't play this game.

The Lady Eleanor School for Girls was a handsome red-brick building, built in the Edwardian style, with a sweeping D-shaped driveway, immaculate lawns, and flower beds given over to daffodils and pink and white hyacinths. The main school block was surrounded by woods and undulating sports fields, in which various acts of lacrosse, hockey, and cross-country running were no doubt perpetrated.

Chef Maurice had decided that the next step in the investigation was to delve into the past of the victim herself. Miranda did not appear to have cultivated many friends on her return to the area, but hopefully here at her alma mater they would be able to find those who could cast some light on her so-far enigmatic character.

"You might be onto something there," Arthur had said, when Chef Maurice had turned up to collect him in his little red Citroën. "These old schools, they're marvellous for promoting staff longevity. You go shooting up from shorts to trousers in a handful of years, but the teachers? Hardly age a dot. Must be all those youthful hormones in the air. I went back a few years ago to visit my old prep school and, you know, they were practically all still there. All in their eighties, mind you, but still going strong. Miss Dickie and her tropical fish collection, and Miss Harrison—boy, I've never seen a woman with such a terrific aim with a nub of chalk . . ."

Now, as they puttered up the drive and followed the signs to the Parents' and Visitors' Car Park, Arthur could feel the concentrated aura of a hundred years of righteous schooling emanating from those red-brick walls. It left him with a sudden urge to pull up his socks and tuck in his shirt.

"So what's our story?" he said, as they strolled through the stone archway into the main Reception, narrowly missing a stampede of ponytailed girls wearing pleated skirts and polo shirts, and all carrying weapons of shin-bruising destruction. "Because I hate to break it to you, but we don't exactly blend in here."

But Chef Maurice was already striding over to the young woman standing at Reception, who was busy sorting a pile of classroom registers into order.

"*Bonjour, mademoiselle.* We talked on the telephone this morning. About a tour of the school?"

"Oh, yes, Mr Manchot, wasn't it? How lovely to meet you. I'm Miss Everwright. You said you were looking for a school for your niece?"

"Oui, for *la petite Arabelle.* Her mother wishes for her to study away from home, and to learn more of the wonderful language of the English."

Arthur turned his chuckle into a hasty cough. He knew for a fact that his friend had no great love of the English language, wonderful or not. Instead, Chef Maurice seemed to positively revel in the cultivation of his impenetrable accent—still thicker, after all these years, than a pair of

129

school dunces—and as yet could not be persuaded that there was no such word in the English language as 'sheeps'.

"How delightful," said Miss Everwright, picking up a pile of papers and scooting out from behind the desk. "We have boarders from all around the world, I'm sure Arabelle would be quite at home here. Were you looking for her to board, or attend as a day pupil?"

"Eh?" Chef Maurice looked to Arthur, who spoke fluent Boarding School Admissions.

"Boarder, at least to start with," said Arthur. "Annabelle's—"

"—*Arabelle's*—"

"—ahem, Arabelle's mother doesn't think that Maurice here is quite up to providing a rounded home life for an eleven-year-old, especially not with a restaurant to run at the same time."

Chef Maurice's moustache bristled indignantly, while Miss Everwright smiled an even brighter smile, full in the knowledge of the hefty additional school fees that came with international boarders.

She handed them each an embossed school brochure and led them through a set of swinging doors and down a long wood-panelled corridor. The walls were hung with rows of long, wide frames containing the annual school photographs—the girls neatly lined up in height order, with the younger ones cross-legged at the front in pinafores and the older ones in green blazers and bowler hats tied with ribbon. As they walked on, the photos turned to sepia, and pigtails and bowl cuts came back into fashion.

Chef Maurice stopped before an old black-and-white photo of a group of girls posed around a silver sporting trophy. "The school, it has many distinguished students from the past, *n'est-ce pas?*"

"Oh, certainly. There was Greta Burroughs, of course, who won the Nobel Prize for Chemistry back in the Fifties. Then there were the Almore sisters, you might have read their books, as well as Ingrid Fullers . . ."

Miss Everwright, eyes shining, proceeded to reel off a long list of notable sportswomen, academics, politicians and businesswomen.

"I believe," said Chef Maurice, as the young woman paused to draw breath, "that Mademoiselle Miranda Matthews from the television was also a student here once?"

Miss Everwright froze. "I'm afraid we're not really allowed to discuss that topic, in light of recent events. I hope you'll understand." Having now laid down the official party line, she lowered her voice, adding: "But, I mean, it's not like you can really stop the girls from spreading things around themselves, what with the way the news is nowadays."

"*Oui*, that is true." Chef Maurice leaned in further. "The . . . incident, it took place on the grounds of the school, am I right?"

Miss Everwright nodded. "On the edge of the grounds, quite far from here, you understand. Thank goodness it was half-term last week, so most of the girls were away visiting their families. But we had a few boarders staying on, and they were here when the police came round. Now, half the girls won't go outdoors, and we can't keep the other half from running down to the creek every chance they get to 'see what else might float up'. Honestly, the ideas they get!"

"Is it true, the rumour I hear that a person was seen running from the creek to the main road, through the school gardens? Just after the hour of the attack?"

"Really?" said Arthur, who hadn't heard anything of the sort.

Miss Everwright looked equally confused. "Oh no, that definitely can't be true. I was here when the police were interviewing our gardeners. They were both out on the back lawn that day, so they'd have seen anyone trying to cut through our land. We've had a lot of nature-lovers trespassing lately—there's apparently some new type of river otter that's turned up on our grounds, *National Geographic* is coming to do a feature next week. Miss Caruthers is getting very angry about it—the trespassers, I mean—so now the gardeners are always on the lookout of anyone suspicious hanging around. They'd definitely have noticed someone cutting up through the grounds. And even if he"—it seemed in Miss Everwright's oestrogen-filled world, all criminals were undoubtedly male—"had tried to go down along the creek instead, over to the woodlands on the other side of our grounds, he'd have been bound to be seen at some point. Our main building overlooks that stretch of the river."

"Ah, and there was no one who saw anything, then?"

"Not a soul. Well, except for Marcia Mendez, who's been telling everyone she saw a black-caped man run across the lawn with a rose in his teeth. But she spent the whole of last term insisting she was engaged to a vampire. So she's not exactly a reliable witness."

They stopped outside a glass-panelled door labelled '*Salle de classe française*'. Inside, thirty heads were bent over thick textbooks, while a middle-aged lady with a pince-nez and red square heels stalked up and down the rows, declaiming in strident tones the proper conjugation of the verb '*dormir* (to sleep)'—while members of the back row appeared to be putting this knowledge to practical application.

"Is there much in the way of staff turnover here?" asked Arthur, as they continued on down the hallway.

"Not at all. We pride ourselves on one of the lowest staff turnovers in the country for a school of this size. Our headmistress, Miss Caruthers, for example, has been here for over forty years."

"Ah, *oui*. She retires this year, is that correct?"

"Yes, that's right," replied Miss Everwright, though a strange look flitted across her face. "And then there's Mr McNutty. He's been the Head of Canteen for almost as long as Miss Caruthers has been here. He'll tell you himself, but he's got the best memory for dates and names I've ever come across. Remembers every pupil who's ever eaten here. At least that's what he claims."

"Ah!" said Chef Maurice, throwing a look at Arthur. "I think we would be most interested in visiting the school dining room."

Miss Everwright nodded. No doubt she had encountered a number of equally food-focused French parents in the past.

"Of course. Now might be a good time, in fact, before lunch break starts." She pushed through another set of swinging doors. "Mr McNutty bakes all our bread on-site, and he's won the county's Best Dinner Lady five times in a row now."

"Impressive," said Arthur. He wondered idly what changes there had been in school catering fashions in the decades since his own days of frozen peas and semolina pudding. On stepping into the dining room, he was therefore pleased to see that, despite some interior designer's best efforts with bright pine benches and abstract wall paintings, the answer was: very little.

Today's blackboard announced such favourites as ploughman's lunch, jam roly-poly, and toad-in-the-hole. (The latter was a particular bugbear of Chef Maurice's, who had encountered grave difficulties in sourcing the necessary amphibians when he had first heard of this British favourite.)

They located Mr McNutty at the back of the kitchens, unloading a tray of steaming wholemeal rolls from a big commercial oven.

"I know who you are," he said, halfway through Miss Everwright's introduction. "You's Mister Maurice, from the restaurant down in Beakley. Took the missus there once, but she had a nasty turn after the sight of all 'em little frogs' legs. Not your fault, though. I told 'er I didn't think *Grenouille* was a place in Switzerland, but sometimes there's no talking to 'er once she's made up 'er mind. So you got a little lass looking to come here, then?"

The story of the relocating niece was quickly rehashed.

"She was here at this weekend," continued Chef Maurice, "and she tells me she most enjoyed the Beakley Spring Fayre. Did you have the chance to attend, *monsieur?*"

"'Fraid not. Kitchen runs all through the holidays. Got the staff to feed, plus a few of the lasses stick around, too far to go home. Some of 'em went over for the Fayre, though. Came back telling me they want a pig roast every Friday now," he said with a grimace, unenthused at the idea of going the whole hog.

Chef Maurice cast a quick look over at Miss Everwright, who was staring speculatively at a tray of chocolate cookies. "You have heard the sad news of Mademoiselle Miranda Matthews, I am sure. Perhaps you remember her, from her days here at the school?"

"'Course I do. Never forget a face, not even when they change their hair and paint their eyes and all that stuff women do. I remember little Miranda all right. Her and Angela—that's Mrs Gifford now, our cookery teacher, funny how these things turn out—those two, they'd always be hanging around 'ere, trying to snitch the pies fresh out the oven, and pestering me for my butter shortbread recipe. Always knew she'd end up doing good for 'erself, our Miranda," he added with some pride.

"And her disposition? Was she a *jeune fille* who caused much trouble, played the tricks?"

"Oh no, I never had any trouble from 'er. Always Mister McNutty this, Mister McNutty that, ever so polite. Face of an angel, too, bless 'er. I did hear there was a few times those two got called up in front of the headmistress, sneaking around after hours when they shouldn't 'ave been, stealing one of the other girls' letters, something like that, but I just call that high spirits. No 'arm in them. At least, back in those days."

"Ah, but later? You heard of trouble caused by Mademoiselle Miranda more recently?"

Mr McNutty stared at Chef Maurice. "You what? Nah, I'm talkin' about Mrs Gifford. You should hear 'er go on now, all high and mighty about her vitamins, and minerals, and government guidelines. Sayin' I should be using less suet in me clootie dumplings! Oh, they all think she's a meek and mild one, but you should 'ave seen her face after I tried putting me famous deep-fried pork pies on the menu. Family recipe, that is. Never did me granny any harm."

"It's a wonder they're all still so slim," commented Arthur, as they headed out of the dining room, battling their way through the incoming tide of Fifth Formers.

"That's what I thought too," said Miss Everwright, "when I first got here, but actually, it's making them eat that's sometimes the problem. They can be surprisingly health-conscious. In fact, last term the older girls were petitioning for a salad and juice bar. I'm sure you can imagine what Mr McNutty said to that."

The next stop was the Home Economics lab, where Angie, somewhat surprised to see her two co-investigators on her home turf, tentatively accepted Chef Maurice's offer to conduct a flambéed apple crêpe demonstration for the class.

The girls, roused from the stupor of attempting to design 'a better mousse', sat up in their seats and eyed this large-moustached intruder with interest.

"Have you heard anything new about last Saturday?" asked Arthur, as he and Angie stood at the back of the room, watching Chef Maurice mix up a large bowl of batter.

A less thoughtful observer might have expected this to take place with a great deal of eggs flying and batter splattering, but they would have been wrong—chefs abhor the wasting of food, and Chef Maurice whisked away at his batter with all the care and attention of a motherly hen.

Thirty pairs of eyes watched in rapt attention.

"I haven't heard much, no," said Angie. "The police came round here, of course, but most of the girls were away, and the ones that weren't were all down at the Fayre."

"Miss Everwright says no one was seen cutting through the grounds that day."

Angie nodded, watching uneasily as Chef Maurice poured a generous measure of Calvados into a big metal ladle. "It really wouldn't make sense to come up through here. Not when whoever it was could have just popped back up to the Fayre and blended in with the rest of the crowd."

There was a *poof* as the alcohol ignited, followed by a burst of applause as Chef Maurice tipped the flaming sauce over the crêpes and caramelised apples. Stools scraped as the class dashed forward, forks at the ready, to get a taste.

"Our work here, it is done," said Chef Maurice, ambling over and handing Angie back her flower-patterned apron.

"Not much news from Angie, I'm afraid," said Arthur, as they stepped out into the hallway, where he found himself counting the number of fire extinguishers hung on the walls nearby. "So where to next?"

"Ah, I think here is our answer."

Miss Everwright was speed walking down the corridor in their direction.

"Miss Caruthers will see you now."

"And so, into the dragon's lair," murmured Arthur.

"Oh!" She looked at him in some surprise. "So you've met her before?"

To label Miss Caruthers' reign over the Lady Eleanor School for Girls as draconian would not be being entirely fair. Though possessing of a sharp tongue, she had never actually been seen to breathe fire, and though she might stalk the midnight corridors with soft shoes and an acute ear tuned for mischief, throwing windows open in the belief that fresh air promoted healthy growth, she seemed little inclined to jump up onto the sill and take to the night skies on leathery wings.

However, when it came to sleeping on a pile of gold, here Miss Caruthers' critics were on potentially firmer ground. It was said that the headmistress of the Lady Eleanor School for Girls kept a shrewd eye on the global economy, and possessed a keen intuition when it came to the most opportune time to increase school fees—while, of course, still inducing in parents a feeling of overwhelming relief to have secured their daughter a place at one of England's most respectable educational establishments.

"Do you really have a niece, Mr Manchot?" was Miss Caruthers' first enquiry, after Miss Everwright had departed.

Chef Maurice contrived to look offended. "*Mais oui*, of course. I have many nieces and nephews."

"I see." Miss Caruthers lowered her glasses half an inch, as a hunter might cock his rifle, and peered severely at her two visitors sat opposite her. "I understand that the unfortunate events of last Saturday's Fayre have Angela quite worked up into a tizzy, but I do not think it's appropriate for you both to be leading her on in this ill-advised manner, believing yourselves capable of doing the job of our country's own police force. And I certainly do not approve of you concocting relatives and wasting my staff's time and energy." She focused her gaze on Arthur. "Really, Mr Wordington-Smythe, I would have expected better of *you*."

Arthur squirmed in his chair and tried to appear contrite, if only for the sake of his position on next year's cake-tasting panel. As he attempted to avoid the headmistress's glare, his eye was caught by a black-and-white photograph on Miss Caruthers' desk showing three young girls, all in Lady Eleanor uniforms, standing before a tall sycamore tree. The youngest of the trio was staring directly at the camera with a familiar piercing gaze.

"Your family have a long history with the school, I see," he said, by way of a conversational sidestep.

Miss Caruthers looked down at the photo, her face softening a fraction. "Yes, all three of us girls were sent here. Deirdre and I only overlapped a few years. She was already in the Sixth Form when I arrived. Caroline was in the year above me."

The name seemed familiar to Arthur. There had been that Winter Jumble Sale down at the village hall, in aid of a leukaemia charity, and he had a vague memory of Miss Caruthers' sister being mentioned.

"Forgive me, is she the one . . . who—"

"Yes, she passed away last year after a long battle with leukaemia. Though sometimes I have to object to that phrase—to employ the word 'battle' gives the suggestion that one has a choice in these matters."

Arthur nodded solemnly, while Chef Maurice, annoyed at the derailment of the conversation at hand, cleared his throat.

"We promise to intrude no further on your school, Madame Caruthers. But while we sit here, perhaps you can tell us more of the character of Mademoiselle Miranda. We understand that she caused some small matters of trouble when she was a student here?"

"My staff clearly talk too much. But yes, she was the worst type of troublemaker, to my mind. And I say that as rather an authority on the subject, after teaching here for over four decades."

"Ah, fights in the changing room, frogs in the water fountains, painting all the teachers' cars bright yellow, that kind of thing?" said Arthur, who'd attended an all-boys establishment.

"I wish," said Miss Caruthers. "Unfortunately, I think you'll find that girls, Mr Wordington-Smythe, prefer a wholly more insidious form of troublemaking. And Miranda was quite the expert. The starting of nasty little rumours, the spread of gossip. Picking up some junior girl as her best friend one week, then spilling all her secrets the next. It causes quite a pernicious effect, to have that type of girl in the year. Though, of course, she wasn't the first of that kind. Nor the last, for that matter."

"And yet, *madame*, you let her continue her studies here?"

"The choice was outside my control. I was Head of Geography at the time. And she had Miss Furlong, my predecessor, completely wrapped around her little finger. And most of the staff, too."

"Ah, *oui*, it is true that Monsieur McNutty speaks quite highly of her."

"Indeed? I'm not surprised. He's been harping on at me to allow him to put on a memorial menu in Miranda's honour. I said it was quite out of the question. I will not have him blowtorching Smarties on these premises."

"*Oui*, that would be most dangerous," said Chef Maurice, who still smelled faintly of Calvados fumes.

"I suppose then," said Arthur, "your feelings on the matter have mellowed since those days, what with Miranda being involved with the Beakley Spring Fayre?"

"Not at all. It was Angela who suggested that Miranda play a role this year. She came to me one day in the staff room, telling me that Miranda was *insistent* on doing some form of demonstration at the Fayre. And wanted to sit on the Bake Off panel. In the end, I relented, if only for Angela's sake—I understood they were planning to set up some little cookery school business together, and the Fayre would be good for their publicity, make Miranda more of a local presence. Oh, don't look so shocked," she added, seeing Arthur's face. "I wouldn't be sitting where I am today if I didn't have a pretty good idea of what my staff are up to. Angela's a good teacher, of course, but I never thought that she'd stay forever. She has more ambition than one might think. I think she'll do very well, going into business."

"Did Mademoiselle Miranda have any other friends from the school in this area?" said Chef Maurice.

"I don't believe so. In those days, most of the girls were boarders like her, so very few settled down locally after they left us. Angela was one of our few day pupils. Her parents ran a farm over near Winchcombe. Now, if that's all"—Miss Caruthers placed her hands on her desk and stood—"I'm afraid I'll have to end our little interview here. I have meetings this afternoon I must prepare for. If you would take my advice, you'd best to leave this matter well alone. You'll find that old debts have a way of being paid in the end, and Miranda Matthews had more than her fair share, I'm sure."

With that, she led them to the door and firmly ushered them out.

"Madame Caruthers, she knows something," said Chef Maurice, as they wandered back to the car.

"Indeed. But any idea what?"

Chef Maurice shook his head. "But, it makes me think of a particular mustard . . ."

"Maurice?"

"*Oui?*"

"Is there *anything* that doesn't make you think about food?"

CHAPTER 9

The Cochon Rouge dinner rush was dialling down when PC Lucy arrived that evening. Chef Maurice, declaring the kitchen safe in his team's capable hands, was in the process of retiring upstairs with a plate of rhubarb crumble and a large jug of custard, to 'contemplate on the case of Mademoiselle Miranda'. After a while, various snores of deep contemplation could be heard through the kitchen ceiling above.

PC Lucy took a seat at the big oak table, a forkful of lemon tart in one hand and a pen in the other.

"Come on, then," she said to Patrick, who was plating up a quartet of marmalade-and-chocolate fondants. "It's not that hard. We've already got the pros written down. So what are the cons of moving jobs?"

Patrick pushed the finished plates towards Dorothy, who scooped them onto a tray and hustled them out into the dining room. "Okay, let's see. The restaurant in the Lake District will probably have less of a local customer base, at least to start with. More tourists, so I'd have to keep the menu a bit more traditional."

"Definitely a con," said PC Lucy, noting this down. Chef Maurice might have been a staunch believer that the only cuisine worth cooking was the one of his native France, but he also possessed the boredom threshold of a sugar-crazed chimpanzee and was tolerant of the occasional bout of experimental or international cuisine onto his menu—as long, of course, as a suitably francophone name for the dish could be concocted. The *porc tiré à la Texane* (pulled pork in a barbeque sauce) had long been a favourite on the lunch specials menu, as well as the *gâteau le meutre par le chocolat* (murder being, according to Chef Maurice, a far more suitable description of the near deadly amount of cocoa in that particular cake).

"Another con, there'd need to be three shifts, to include the hotel breakfast as well. That'd definitely be a pain. And it'll be harder to recruit up there, I reckon."

PC Lucy nodded and added this to the list. "Anything else?"

Patrick rubbed his nose, leaving a tantalising smudge of chocolate across one cheek. "No, I think that's it."

"You sure?"

"I think so."

He turned to check on some dehydrating olives in the oven behind him, while PC Lucy gripped her pen and held back the urge to throw it at his (admittedly rather fine) blue-and-white-checked behind.

The cheek! To not even include 'my girlfriend lives right here in the Cotswolds' as a disadvantage of moving several hundred miles north? She knew Patrick set great store by his career, and painful experiences with certain exes had taught her to never get in the way of a man and his métier—but, really! Just the other week, he'd been dropping hints about the prospect of them moving in together.

At least, that's what she'd thought at the time, when the subject of his flat's rent coming up for renewal had floated across their conversational path. He'd made a passing comment about how he might prefer not to renew and to look for another, bigger, place instead.

Now, though, she wondered if Mrs Merland hadn't already had a quiet word in her son's ear, and if the whole rent discussion had been his subtle way of preparing PC Lucy for news of his imminent relocation . . .

Patrick was still crouched down by the oven. She shoved the list across the table. "Here you go. It's all down here. I'm sure it won't be a very hard decision."

With as much calm as she could muster, she stalked out of the back door and down into the village.

Back to her flat. Alone.

Patrick watched, puzzled, as PC Lucy disappeared out of the back door.

"Do you think she looked a bit annoyed about something?" he asked Alf, who was podding a bowl of just-blanched broad beans for the next day's lunch menu.

"Dunno," said Alf, who was of the private opinion that Patrick's girlfriend lived her life on a tide of barely concealed rage, and the less directed at him, Alf, the better.

"She was pretty insistent on me doing that list. Do you think it's something I said?"

He looked down at the piece of paper, which was divided into two columns, each filled with PC Lucy's neat handwriting. To his surprise, the 'pros' column, in favour of relocating, was rather longer than he remembered.

Dorothy, returning with a tray of rattling crockery, glanced over his shoulder.

"Oooo, dearie me! You're in trouble now," was her pronouncement.

"What? Why?"

"You've gone and left our Lucy right off the list. I imagine she took off pretty fast after that." She elbowed Patrick in the ribs. "Am I right?"

"She said something before about an early start to-morrow. And I didn't put her on the list *on purpose*."

Dorothy folded her arms over her ample bosom and tilted her head with a 'try me' expression.

"See, I can't let her think I'd choose to stay in Beakley because of her," explained Patrick, "or else she might feel . . . well, obliged to carry on going out with me. I want her to feel free to end things whenever she wants, instead of feeling guilt-tripped into us staying together because I chose to turn down the head chef job."

Alf nodded along to this display of proto-male reasoning at its finest.

"And what did she say about this little list of yours, then?" said Dorothy.

"She said it looked like an easy decision," said Patrick slowly.

They all looked down at the lengthy 'pros' column.

"Cor!" said Alf. "Do you think she said that, because, like, she actually *wants* you to go?"

The two chefs stared at each other in horror.

Dorothy, eyes rolling, picked up her tray and dumped the contents in the sink.

It was true what they said. Behind every great man, you found an extremely perplexed woman, wondering what the heck had happened.

The next day dawned fine and clear across the rolling Cotswold hills. Down by Warren's Creek, wisps of clouds reflected off the placid waters, and the weeping willows dappled the sunlight as it fell on the path running alongside the bank.

By co-conspiratorial agreement, Arthur, Chef Maurice and Angie had convened at this early hour to take another look at the scene of the crime.

"Pretty little spot, isn't it?" said Arthur, standing on the jetty, hands in pockets. In accordance to the day's watery theme, he was wearing navy-blue boat shoes and a striped linen jacket.

"You're not the only one who thinks so," said Angie, as she bent down to peep under a nearby bush. "In the summer, we get all kinds of people trespassing on the grounds here, coming to sit and have their picnics. That's not so bad. It's when we get couples who come here to . . . well . . ."

"Spoon?" suggested Arthur.

(Chef Maurice, sitting nearby, furrowed his brow. He was unsure what cutlery had to do with the current discussion.)

"Near enough. And it's not as if they don't know they're on our grounds. Sometimes the girls come across them, and, well . . . let's just say that Miss Pearce, our Biology teacher, says she gets quite a lot of questions afterwards." Angie's cheeks, Arthur noticed, had gone quite pink.

He glanced over at Chef Maurice, who was sitting at the edge of the clearing on a rickety moss-covered bench, his pork-pie hat across his face.

"Maurice, are you going to help us search, or just sit there having a kip?"

That hat was raised one inch. "I am not a kipper, *mon ami*. I simply reflect on the puzzle before us. It is clear that Mademoiselle Miranda was one who made both enemies and trouble quite easily. But who is the enemy this time? And what is their motive?"

"We haven't looked much into the money angle, yet," said Arthur, using a branch to poke through a patch of soft earth. "Miranda was quite high up in the last *England Observer* Rich List, if I recall correctly."

"Ah, so again we look to the aunt of Mademoiselle Miranda?"

"Nonsense," said Angie, appearing back out of the trees, a leaf stuck behind her ear. "Anyway, I managed to speak to Miranda's solicitors yesterday. They said her aunt's not even been in the country these last few weeks. She's been on a Mediterranean cruise since the end of March. So I hope that puts paid to your theory. The thought of being suspicious of a nice little old lady like her!"

"Humph." Chef Maurice disagreed with this notion. In his experience, little old ladies were perfectly placed for the execution of all manner of criminal activities, starting with being the most miserly tippers at the restaurant.

"*Un moment*. How is it that the solicitors, they spoke with you? They were most rude to me when I telephoned to them!" Lawyers, in his mind, had no right withholding information from his investigation, and he had told them as much. (Oddly enough, the line had cut out at that point, and no one had picked up for a good hour afterwards. He hoped nothing too untoward had happened at their offices, and had made a mental note to pop round to check next time he was in Cowton. And to continue his complaint in person, of course.)

"Oh, it was only because they had to speak with me. They told me Miranda left a small amount of money to the business, according to the way the agreement was drawn up. Rory insisted we had a proper contract, you see, so that if either of us pulled out, the other could continue the project. Of course, we never imagined a situation like this."

"So, the money, does it mean you may now continue in the bid?"

Angie nodded. "It's enough to pay the rent for the first two years, and for most of the refurbishment work. I might still need to take out a loan, but it means I'm definitely not withdrawing the application now." She spoke brusquely, as if not wanting to dwell on nor sound too happy about this unexpected silver lining.

The next twenty minutes were spent combing the ground, or at least peering intently at it and prodding it with long sticks. Angie set to work along the downstream bank, towards the school, with a remit to look out for further clues that may have washed up over the last few days, while Chef Maurice and Arthur took the westward path—the path that Miranda had presumably walked that last fateful Saturday.

"I still can't understand," said Arthur, "why our attacker decided to throw away the murder weapon into the bushes. I mean, they could have just as easily thrown it into the creek."

"Ah, but the crime, perhaps it was the thought of the moment. In a panic, the murderer throws down the pipe and runs fast away."

"Possible. Though that rather suggests our soon-to-be murderer just happened to be strolling along here, carrying around a handy piece of iron piping. A bit too much co-incidence there, in my opinion." Arthur stopped and cocked his head. "Did you hear that?"

"*Comment?*"

"Sounded like a car starting up. Over that way." He waved a hand towards the wooded slope, which led up to the road.

"And so? Cars, they must start, before they can go. You must learn to concentrate more, *mon ami*."

Arthur thought about explaining that the car they had just heard had been a jolly interesting car to hear, sounding a good deal like a 1960s Jaguar E-Type—a car that Arthur had insisted would be a rock-solid investment, but that Meryl had dismissed as 'far too windy for the motorways'. However, given that Chef Maurice only cared about vintage when it came to matters such as wine and, occasionally, tinned sardines, he decided to let the matter drop.

"Never mind. So you agree that the crime was most likely premeditated?"

"*Oui*, I think you have reason. I have thought for some time, too, that this was no accident or sudden act. It is too clean. That no one, at an event of hundreds, saw anything of suspicion? Much planning had to be made. Perhaps long before the crime itself."

By now they had strayed quite far from the creek, lost in the criss-cross of tiny woodland paths.

"It's no good," said Arthur, stopping and looking around. "There's too many paths. Anyone coming from the Fayre could have climbed over that joke of a fence at any point along here. It'll take days to go over this whole area."

"Ah, then it is good that we will not have to. See this. Our prey, they have left us a trail." Chef Maurice turned around from his examination of a prickly gorse bush, and held up something white and fluffy in his hand.

It was a fake rabbit tail.

CHAPTER 10

By unspoken agreement, neither Chef Maurice nor Arthur mentioned the discovery of the rabbit tail to Angie. Until they identified the bunny it belonged to, it seemed cruel to put her through any unnecessary worry.

Chef Maurice, for his part, already had ideas as to his preferred guilty party. Mayor Gifford had recently hosted a small dinner at Le Cochon Rouge for some local business owners, a dinner at which Miss Karole Linton had also been in attendance. The research assistant had shown great taste in her menu choice, eschewing some of the more prosaic offerings in favour of a dish of *andouillettes* in a mustard sauce, paired with a creamy white Burgundy of her choosing from one of the lesser-known communes.

No woman, he said to Arthur, with such a discerning palate would choose to commit murder with the aid of a length of iron pipe.

Mayor Gifford, on the other hand, had ordered the rump steak with matchstick fries, and accompanied his entire meal with several pints of run-of-the-barley-mill beer. And he'd ordered his steak *extremely* well done. Here was a man capable of the most heinous of crimes.

"I don't know, old chap," said Arthur, as they stood outside the Cowton Police Station, waiting for PC Lucy to turn up for her morning shift. "Chops to the lady for ordering the offal sausage and all, but it's not what I'd call conclusive evidence."

"Bah, you will see," said Chef Maurice, sipping on his extra-large cup of coffee. He gave a little shudder. The memory of the mayor sawing away at what had once been twelve ounces of prime Aberdeen rump still haunted him on bad nights.

PC Lucy was not in a good mood when she rounded the corner to find two early morning visitors waiting on the steps.

"Look, this isn't like the doctors," she said, unlocking the door to the main office. "You can't just turn up and expect to be seen. We're really busy this week, you know."

Unfortunately, her point was not much helped by the complete absence of her other colleagues who, revelling in the fact that Chief Inspector Grant was still on his Easter holidays and that the weather continued to be unseasonably fine, had all decided that Cowton's picturesque High Street could do with some gentle patrolling.

"We are in need of the photographs from the Spring Fayre," said Chef Maurice, bouncing up and down on his feet with an urgency not usually seen, apart from first thing in the morning as Le Cochon Rouge's coffee machine spluttered to life.

"And what exactly do you need them for?"

Chef Maurice thrust out a paper bag printed with the logo of the coffee shop round the corner.

"Look, you can't just sweet-talk me into helping you with a blueberry muffin—" PC Lucy stopped, frowning at the contents of the bag.

"We found it caught in a bush, in the woods near where Mademoiselle Miranda was found," explained Chef Maurice. He sat down in PC Alistair's chair and gave her an expectant look.

Wordlessly, PC Lucy booted up her own computer. While she waited, she transferred the tail into a more suitable bag. It appeared to be a cheap costume item, its synthetic fibres already starting to moult.

Chef Maurice and Arthur drew their chairs up either side of her.

"They've all been sorted into time order," said PC Lucy, clicking through the folder and stopping at every photo of Mayor Gifford or Karole Linton. There were quite a number of each, owing to the mayor's upcoming political campaign and Miss Karole Linton's aforementioned photogenic assets.

One photo showed both bunny-eared parties from behind, deep in conversation with a local magistrate.

"Eleven fifteen," said Arthur, pointing at the timestamp. "Both tails still present."

They continued onwards through the photos of Miranda's cookery demo, the long queues for lunch, and then the sight of the eager crowds converging on the Bake Off tent. There were, however, no rabbit costumes in sight.

"Maybe we should try the videos," said PC Lucy. "We've had members of the public sending in their recordings. There might—"

"Wait, go back! *Regarde*." Chef Maurice jabbed a finger at the screen, which showed a pair of boys with faces painted, one as a lion and the other, who presumably had drawn the shorter straw, as a wardrobe. But in the background, leaning over to paint more swirls onto a little girl sitting on a stool, was Miss Karole Linton and her pert behind.

Missing one fluffy bunny tail.

There was a minor kerfuffle as both PC Lucy and Chef Maurice attempted to get out through the main office door at the same time. A few moments later, passers-by were treated to the sight of a blonde policewoman chasing a large, walrus-moustached gentleman down the street and all the way into the Cowton Town Hall.

The pair's progress, however, was impeded by the stout security-guard-cum-receptionist, whose job it was to deter unannounced visitors from pushing their way through into the offices of the mayor and his staff.

"But it is of a matter of the most urgency!" insisted Chef Maurice, thumping his hands on the desk.

The man inspected PC Lucy's badge, then grudging allowed her to pass. She was ushered into the mayor's offices, panting but triumphant, while Chef Maurice and Arthur—who'd turned up a few minutes later, cup of coffee in hand—were left in the foyer, to argue their case with the Hulk at Reception.

Mayor Gifford's outer office was a sunny room on the ground floor, filled with mismatched desks and a maze of filing cabinets.

"Can I help you?" said a grey-bunned lady to PC Lucy's left. She had a raspy voice, and was engaged in stuffing election flyers into a stack of printed envelopes.

"I'm looking for Miss Karole Linton."

Karole, sat at a desk half-hidden behind a nest of filing cabinets, looked up in surprise.

"Yes?" she said, standing up. She was wearing a royal-blue shift dress, cut in that straight-up, straight-down fashion that only looks good on the extremely slim, and her hair was pinned back in an elegant chignon.

"Is there somewhere we can speak in private?"

A few nearby heads tilted up in interest. Karole nodded, still looking politely puzzled, and led PC Lucy across to a door on the far side of the room. "We can use the meeting room here. Rory doesn't need it until one."

The mayor's meeting room was small but lavishly appointed, hung with sombre oil paintings and furnished with a heavy mahogany table. High up on a corner shelf, a marble bust of some notable Cowton personage glared blindly down at them.

"Do you mind if I open a window?" said Karole. "It gets

rather stuffy in here with the sun coming in all morning." She walked over to one of the sash windows and lifted it open with both hands, with surprising strength for a girl who looked like she ate celery sticks for all three meals, noted PC Lucy.

"How well did you know Miranda Matthews, Miss Linton?"

"We'd never met properly," came Karole's prompt reply. "She came here once for a meeting with Rory. About an application for the old cookery school site on the High Street. Other than that, I don't think we—"

There was a knock at the door and Mr Paul Whittaker stuck his long face around.

"Good afternoon, Constable," he said, nodding at PC Lucy. "I understand you wished to speak to the mayor on some matter? I'm afraid he's still in meetings, but if there's anything I can do instead?" He glanced over at Karole, clearly displeased at the sight of one of his mayoral staff in conversation with the police.

"I'm afraid it's something I need to speak about in person with the mayor, but thank you."

Mr Whittaker sniffed, then nodded and retracted his head.

Karole Linton folded her hands in her lap. "As I was saying, that was the only time I properly met her. If you want to know more about the cookery school bids, you probably should speak to Mr Whittaker. He's the one who dealt with all the applications."

"I came to speak to you about this," said PC Lucy, pulling out the clear bag containing the fluffy rabbit tail.

"May I?" Karole picked up the bag and turned it over in her hands. "This isn't mine, if that's what you came to ask me," she said finally. "Mine was a little more cream-coloured, and came with a big white pin. This one's the type that sews on, you can see the threads there."

PC Lucy peered at the bag. True, there were a few short threads poking out from the seam of the tail . . .

"Anyway, I know where my one is," continued Karole. "Rory has it."

"I'm sorry?"

"It's now on Rory's costume. He lost his during the Fayre. I remember, it was when I was helping out in the face-painting tent at lunchtime, and Angela, Rory's wife, came up to me and said I'd better give him the tail from my costume, because it was more important for his to look proper than mine."

PC Lucy looked at Karole Linton's smooth expression. Either the girl was an experienced liar, or she was actually telling the truth. No matter either way; her statement would be easy enough to check up on.

"It was a terrible costume anyway," Karole added. "I mean, my one."

"Why did you choose it, then?" said PC Lucy, vaguely curious.

"Let's just say it was a drunken bet gone wrong."

"Oh." PC Lucy had trouble imagining Karole doing

anything on a dare, let alone getting sloshed enough to agree to it. "Well, thank you for your time. You've been very helpful."

"No problem. Though I still don't quite see what any of this has to do with Miranda Matthews, I'm afraid."

"This tail piece was found in the woods near Warren's Creek, not far from where the body of Miranda Matthews was discovered last Saturday."

Karole's eyes widened and her lips parted in a silent 'O'.

PC Lucy watched her for a few moments, but no further comment seemed forthcoming. So, with a polite nod, she collected her notebook and the tail and let herself out.

As the door swung shut, she took one final look at the young woman, still sat at the big table, her thin fingers gripped tightly in her lap, staring at the wall opposite. She appeared to be thinking. Hard.

Arthur and Chef Maurice had settled themselves down on a park bench, stretched out their legs and were now enjoying a spot of mild April sunshine. The bench itself was located directly under the window to Mayor Gifford's meeting room—a not entirely serendipitous occurrence, as they had taken a stroll around the Town Hall gardens in search of this very eventuality.

Are they still in there? Arthur scribbled in his notebook and held it up to his friend.

Chef Maurice shrugged, then pulled out a wood-handled metal spatula from his jacket. He gave it a few buffs on his sleeve, then raised the implement above his head. Arthur caught a glimpse of a shiny auburn head in the mirrored surface, but no sign of PC Lucy.

Back to the police station? wrote Arthur.

Chef Maurice gave this a moment's contemplation, then nodded. However, they were both stopped, mid-buttock-rise, by the sound of a door slamming above them and a male voice raised in anger.

"What the hell were you doing, having the police in here like that? Did you think about what it's going to look like to the press?"

"They're the police, Rory, not the paparazzi. For goodness' sake, you can't just fob them off with a 'no comment'." Karole's voice was equally sharp.

"And now they're asking me to come down to the station, some nonsense about a rabbit's tail."

"The police found the tail from your costume, down in the woods where Miranda Matthews was found."

There was a short silence. And then:

"And what does that have to do with anything? Some kid probably pinched it off me when I wasn't looking. I know they had some kind of game going, running up and tugging on the damn thing all day long. There was something bloody magnetic about the thing. I had little old ladies coming up to me and giving it a tug, and I swear I even caught Paul having a go at one point. I told Angie it was a ridiculous costume. Anyway, one of those kids probably pulled it off and threw it into the woods. Probably thought it'd be funny."

"So that's what happened?" She spoke quietly, but her tone was accusatory.

"Careful, Karole," growled the mayor.

There was the sound of a chair scraping back. "Careful? Me? When I've been telling you to be nothing *but* careful—"

"All right, all right, enough! I've got to go down to the police station to speak to that policewoman, God help me. I'll talk to you when I get back. Fine mess you've landed me in."

"Me? What on earth do you mean by—" But the door slammed again.

Arthur gestured urgently to Chef Maurice. Together, crouching low to avoid being noticed, they hobbled off to report this latest exchange to PC Lucy.

From across the Town Hall gardens, their departure was watched by a young mother walking with her little girl.

"See over there, dear," said the mother. "If you don't sit up straight, you'll end up all bent over like those gentlemen there. And we don't want that now, do we?"

"Looks like Karole was telling the truth," said PC Lucy, sitting back in her swivel chair.

"Play it again," demanded Chef Maurice, leaning in closer to the screen. He and Arthur had spent the last twenty minutes waiting impatiently outside the police station, while PC Lucy dealt with a red-faced and extremely unhelpful Mayor Gifford, who'd finally stormed off with

163

dire threats to phone up the Chief Inspector at his Corfu holiday villa and get him to 'put his damn staff on a leash'.

PC Lucy hit 'play' and the video jumped to life once more. It showed a wobbly close-up of a little boy wearing a red cape, with a petulant expression on his frosting-covered mouth.

"Come on, Billy, smile over here, show Mummy what you're eating," cajoled a sugary voice from off-camera.

But little Billy seemed more interested in the antics of the giant furry rabbit in the distance. "Look, Mummy! She's stealing his bunny tail! Can I have a bunny tail too?"

"Don't be silly, darling, she's helping him pin it back on. Like pinning the tail on the donkey. See, he's all fixed now. And Superman doesn't have a bunny tail, now, does he?"

In the background, as Billy contemplated his bunny-tail-less future, Mayor Gifford twisted around to inspect Angie's work, nodded briefly at her, then walked off, tail bobbing, while Angie pulled herself to her feet and dusted the grass off her long skirt.

PC Lucy paused the video.

"But it makes no sense," said Arthur, voicing the thought they all shared. "What on earth would Mayor Gifford have to gain by murdering Miranda Matthews?"

"You did tell me his wife has inherited some money from Miranda," said PC Lucy.

"Only for the use of the cookery school. She can't touch the money herself. And Rory Gifford's not exactly known to be hard up. The whole scenario is ridiculous."

PC Lucy thought about Angie Gifford's rather worn tweed skirt in the video. No, the mayor did not seem like a man who would spend a lot on his wife, let alone set about to murder her best friend in the aim of small monetary gain.

"Bof, it is clear. Monsieur Gifford must be arrested and put to the questioning."

"I'm afraid that's out of the question. We don't have nearly enough to go on." PC Lucy dreaded to think what Chief Inspector Grant would have to say, coming back from his holidays to find the Mayor of Cowton down in the cells because of the lightest of circumstantial evidence. "Plus, there's no *motive* here."

"Hmm, you are correct. A motive is required." Chef Maurice stopped as he noticed the large-lens camera sitting on PC Sara's desk. "Aha! The camera of Mademoiselle Miranda. What happened of the pictures inside it?"

"Miranda must have used a new memory card, or wiped it recently. There were only two photos, taken on the Saturday morning of the Fayre down by Warren's Creek. Both," she added, before Chef Maurice could get excited, "of a family of river otters."

Chef Maurice paused. "Otter? That is a type of bird, perhaps?"

A quick trawl of the Internet produced several photographs of the water-loving mammal in question.

"Ah, *une loutre*! Of the river. But for me, I am in preference of the *loutre* of the sea. They have, I am told, a great appreciation of seafood. Come, I show you."

Another quick online foray produced a wildlife video of a group of sea otters, enjoying their dinner of fresh crab and other maritime bounty. They were awfully cute, PC Lucy had to admit.

"But, to return to the investigation," said Chef Maurice, after the fifth consecutive video, "it seems now that our task is to discover the motive of Monsieur le mayor. And for that, *mademoiselle*, you may leave it to us."

With this gallant pronouncement, Chef Maurice got up and strutted out of the office. Arthur gave PC Lucy a helpless little shrug, then followed his friend outside.

PC Lucy turned back to her desk. In circumstances such as these, she found it was best not to pry too deeply into Chef Maurice's plans. But she set her phone to ringer, just in case the pair should get themselves arrested for stalking Mayor Gifford all around Cowton.

She stared unseeingly at the screen. What had Miranda really been doing down at Warren's Creek that day? The pictures from her camera suggested a spot of wildlife photography, but it was no otter, no matter how camera-shy, who had clubbed her over the head with a length of iron piping.

As for Mayor Gifford, what had he been up to, sneaking around in the woods that very same morning? The idea that his being there had nothing to do with Miranda could be dismissed as far too much of a coincidence. But if he wasn't involved in the murder, why hadn't he owned up to being down there in the first place?

She clicked on a video of a young sea otter ferociously bashing a clam against a wall of rock, without much result.

It was, she thought, a rather good metaphor for how she was beginning to feel about the whole Miranda Matthews case.

It had not been difficult to wrangle a dinner invitation out of Angie for that evening, which came as a pleasant surprise to both Arthur and Chef Maurice.

Food critics and professional chefs both suffer from a below-average number of dinner invitations from friends and acquaintances, due to fear of criticism, dissatisfaction, and, in the case of Chef Maurice in particular, having their larders severely depleted and their drinks cupboards emptied of the good brandy.

Perhaps Angie would have thought twice about her invitation had she known that the pair's plans included breaking into her husband's home study and subjecting it to a thorough search for 'murderous clues'. However, as such, she gave them the time of half past seven and begged them not to bring anything along; it would just be a simple dinner, rustled up from whatever she had in the fridge and pantry.

Thus, at seven thirty on the dot—Arthur being a stickler for punctuality—they deposited themselves on the bristly doormat outside the Giffords' residence, a detached mock-Tudor house situated in one of Cowton's more affluent areas. The rest of the street was dominated by newly built, honey-stoned Cotswold cottages, and spring flowers bloomed on the grass verges by the roadside.

"You're right on time. Do come inside," said Angie, as she swung open the door. "Oh, you really shouldn't have," she added, graciously accepting the bottle of Bordeaux from Chef Maurice's outstretched hands, as well as the glossy box of chocolates that Arthur had liberated from Meryl's not-so-secret stash.

She led them through to the back of the house, which had been converted into a kitchen-cum-dining-area—an abomination, thought Arthur, that was all the rage nowadays in modern homes. He had also observed, these last few years, that kitchen design had become something of a lesson in landform geography, with islands, peninsulas and (in one particular high-end case) whole archipelagos sprouting up from the rustic Italian tile floors.

"I'm afraid Rory won't be joining us," said Angie, peering into the oven at a large casserole dish. "He has to attend a dinner for the Cowton Small Business Association."

"Ah, that is a shame," said Chef Maurice, who, with Arthur, had spent the afternoon flipping through the local event listings to ascertain that Mayor Gifford would, indeed, be otherwise occupied this evening.

As they settled down around the table with aperitifs in hand, Mayor Gifford popped his blond head into the kitchen and bestowed a megawatt smile on his two visitors, on the off-chance they might be members of his voting public. He was accompanied by a dour-faced Paul Whittaker, who was carrying a briefcase and wearing the look of a man condemned to an evening of jovial company, when he would much rather be at home enjoying a rereading of the *Iliad* in the original Ancient Greek.

"Sorry I can't stay for dinner. I'm sure Angie has cooked up a feast, as she always does. Has she been showing off all her new gadgets? Not that anyone knows what half these buttons do, least of all the lady of the house." Mayor Gifford planted a kiss on his wife's cheek, then headed for the door. "Don't forget, Go With Gifford!"

"I must congratulate you on a most pleasing kitchen," said Chef Maurice, looking around in approval at the solid beech countertops and pastel-blue cupboards. From out in the hallway, they heard the front door bang shut.

"Actually, it was all Rory's choice," said Angie, pulling a pan off the stove to check on the new potatoes. "I quite fancied one of those modern-style kitchens, they're so practical and easy to clean, but Rory insisted we go rustic. Said it would go down better with the voters, when the papers come to take pictures in here. Still," she said, patting the front of the stainless steel oven set high in the wall, "I got my way when it came to this one."

"Ah, *quelle merveille!*" Chef Maurice got up to peer in admiration at the range of shiny controls. "It does the injection of the steam, *oui*?"

"That's right. And has the temperature probe function for roasting. I even made baguettes in it the other day, using the stone base, you can just about see it in there. It's all a matter of the right humidity levels . . ."

Chef Maurice nodded along politely as Angie expounded her theories about crust-to-crumb ratios and bread baking temperatures. For the sake of their upcoming plans to raid Mayor Gifford's study, he was on his best behaviour, managing to avoid any comment on the peculiar English obsession with home breadmaking, when every Frenchman knew that the best way to obtain a perfectly made baguette was to simply pop down to the local boulangerie.

Arthur, leaning back in his chair, glanced out into the dark garden beside him, accessible through a set of mock-Tudor bi-fold doors. Dusk had fallen, and the only light source came from the kitchen, flooding a pale glow across the patio and grass. A set of nightmare-esque shapes at the back of the lawn caught his eye. He blinked, and the strange objects reconciled themselves into a paint-splattered ladder, various lengths of sawn-off timber, an old cast-iron Victorian stove, parts strewn all around, and a cluster of garden gnomes—all of whom were, oddly enough, blond.

"Oh, don't look at that mess," said Angie, waving an oven glove towards the garden. "It's all the rubbish from the old kitchen. The builders keep saying they'll be back to pick it up, but the way things are going, it'll be Christmas by the time they come."

Over a dinner of olive-oil-poached sea trout with garlic-and-dill-infused crème fraîche sauce, Angie filled them in on her own investigations. She'd returned to Miranda's flat that afternoon in search of further clues, but to her dismay, the police had been there since, this time conducting a far more thorough clear-out.

"I mean, they already took her computer the first time, but this time they took all her paper files, all the Little Cowton Kitchen documents, even her photography equipment. I do hope they'll be careful with it all."

"Sounds like the police might be finally taking a look at the cookery school angle," said Arthur.

"If they do, they only follow behind in our steps," huffed Chef Maurice. He turned to Angie. "Tell me, did Mademoiselle Miranda come often to your house here? She and Monsieur Gifford, they were also on the good terms?"

"Miranda and Rory? I'm afraid they didn't really get along. I mean, they were perfectly nice to each other in company. I thought Miranda, especially, was making a big effort to try and get to know him, but Rory didn't really take it the right way. He'd say things like, 'Why does she want to know where I play golf at, and what restaurants I go to?' I tried to tell him she was just being friendly, but it wasn't much good. I think he never really approved of me being friends with 'a celebrity' like Miranda." Angie's cheeks turned pink. "He said she didn't get the right sort of press, and he didn't like us—I mean, me and Miranda— being seen together in public. I know this next election is a huge stepping stone in Rory's career, but I still don't think he needed to be so serious about it all. In the end, we mostly met at Miranda's flat to work on the cookery school. Less fuss all round, that way."

For dessert, Angie coaxed her new oven into producing a picture-perfect lemon soufflé, its edges sharp and crisp as a new twenty-pound note.

"Simply marvellous. Best dessert I've had in ages," said Arthur, folding his napkin beside his empty ramekin, while Chef Maurice expressed his concerns about the whereabouts of the second portions.

"Oh, you flatter me, really!" said Angie, smiling as she collected up the empty dishes.

Chef Maurice furrowed his brow, and Arthur was required to ram his toe against the chef's ankle before he opened his mouth to explain that he was not, in fact, joking about seconds.

"So nice to serve dinner to such a good pair of appetites," Angie continued, from over by the sink. "That's why I could never work as a chef like you, Maurice. I like to see the end results when it comes to my work. That's the nice thing about teaching, you get to see the girls grow up over the years. I don't think I could stand being cooped up in the kitchens, with no idea what was going on out front. I'd want to be out there too, standing and watching over the poor diners as they ate!"

As she filled the sink with hot soapy water, Arthur and Chef Maurice exchanged a silent nod. The covert operation portion of the evening had arrived.

Chef Maurice, claiming he could not live with himself

to see Angie do all the washing up after producing such a fine meal, took the sponge from her hands and commandeered the sink area. Soon, soap suds were flying and Angie stood at the ready, tea towel in hand, as the onslaught of clean crockery began.

Chef Maurice had, correctly, deduced that Angie was the type of woman who knew the exact latitude and longitude for every piece of cookery equipment in her domain, and so he took great pains to conduct his washing up in as haphazard a manner as possible, such that Angie was forced to rush to and fro across the kitchen, stowing away each item with care before the next came shooting out from the sink.

Amidst this whirl of activity, Arthur backed quietly out of the room, mumbling something about a search for the bathroom, then tiptoed across the hallway into Mayor Gifford's study. The mayor had apparently been taking classes from the Henry VIII school of interior design— there was copious wood-panelling, a fireplace fit for a roast hog, and all that was missing was tapestries on the walls and a stag's head over the mantelpiece.

Donning a pair of leather gloves, Arthur hurried over to Mayor Gifford's king-sized desk. He wasn't sure what he was looking for, but a man's desk drawers seemed a reasonable place to begin.

As he passed the bookcase, he stopped to examine one of the leather-bound volumes at random (you never knew what someone might be hiding in a hollowed-out hardback), only to find that the entire shelf was filled with cardboard replicas, of the type found adorning the cabinets in those cut-price furniture warehouses.

For Arthur, an inveterate bibliophile, this was reason enough to start harbouring deep suspicions about the moral fibre of Cowton's mayor.

The top desk drawer was full of stationery odds and ends, while the middle one contained a thick folder of newspaper clippings, all featuring the desk's owner in various commanding poses. So far, so unincriminating.

The bottom drawer, however, revealed a large brown envelope, hidden under a pile of magazines for the discerning gentleman. The envelope was addressed to one Mayor Gifford, with no address and no postmark.

Arthur eased the envelope open. It was empty, apart from a scrap of notepaper bearing the following missive:

Plenty more where these came from . . . I'll be seeing you soon, lover boy . . .

The note was signed off with a curly M.M. and a red lipstick kiss.

CHAPTER 11

In Chef Maurice's opinion, the world of policing operated at a pace of mind-boggling slowness. His own customers, he told PC Lucy, would have been completely up in arms if *he* took that long to get tangible results onto a warm plate and out into the dining room.

However, this reasoning had held little sway with the policewoman, who had been roused from a quiet evening in bed with a good novel to be regaled with tales of his and Arthur's high derring-do in the lair of the philandering Mayor Gifford.

She'd listened, bookmark in hand, then firmly instructed them to their respective beds, forbidding them on pain of pain from conducting any more undercover missions for the remainder of the night, and grudgingly promising to look into matters first thing the following morning.

The next morning came, after a fitful night's rest for Chef Maurice—his mind had been racing at such a pace that it had taken him a whole five minutes to fall asleep, even with the help of a dose of single malt whisky—but when he got down to the kitchens, he found himself facing a form of culinary conundrum that took his mind off the Miranda Matthews case altogether.

He sat at the kitchen table, staring down at a square white plate displaying a slab of sickly-looking mackerel, hacked into zigzag slices, sitting in a pool of what might have been its own congealed blood, but was more likely some form of raspberry or cherry coulis. Around the plate, dotted like remnants from the bottom of a fridge, were tiny cubes of orange jelly, a wrinkled black olive or two, and bright green blobs of what looked like cottage cheese that had just returned from a visit to a nuclear reactor.

He looked up into Alf's hopeful face.

"This . . . dish, it is all your own creation?"

Alf nodded vigorously, while Patrick, face impassive, stood off to one side with his arms folded.

"It is, um, *très inventif.* The colours, the arrangement. *Oui*, I am . . . most impressed."

Having run out of words with which to stall the inevitable, Chef Maurice picked up his fork and speared a slice of mackerel, an orange cube and an olive, then dragged the combination through the vivid red sauce. With a look to the heavens, he took a deep breath and shovelled the whole thing into his mouth.

"Mmmmph!"

"Is it okay, chef?"

Cheeks bulging, Chef Maurice gave his commis chef a desperate thumbs up.

"You sure, chef?"

There was a gulping noise, like a tennis ball being sucked down a pipe.

"Truly . . . excellent," he coughed. "The cherry sauce, perhaps a little too sharp, you must use more sugar. But . . . *oui*," he said, watching Patrick's face out of the corner of his eye, "this is . . . very good. I am very happy with your work."

At this moment, the crunch of gravel outside indicated a vehicle pulling up in the backyard.

"Ah, Patrick, that must be Monsieur Royston with our delivery of meat. If you will go to aid him . . ."

After Patrick had disappeared outside to help lug in the cold boxes, Chef Maurice whipped around to face his commis chef.

"Tell me. It was Patrick, *n'est-ce pas*, who made the recipe for this dish?"

"Er . . ."

"Bah! Come. It is not possible for anyone without a great talent to invent a dish of such"—Chef Maurice shuddered—"unnatural joining of flavours. This is the work of one chef, and one chef only."

"Well, he did give me a bit of a hand with the—"

"Hah! So, Patrick wishes to play a game of the culinary chicken? Then he will have his game!" He strode over to the shelves along the back wall, grabbed down a decanter of cognac and poured himself a large measure. "Ah, that is much better."

"Morning," said PC Lucy, ducking through the back door, closely followed by Patrick with a whole lamb carcass over one shoulder. "Maurice, are you and Arthur free this morning? I've got an interview with someone I thought you might want to meet."

"Ah, so you have made the arrest of Monsieur le mayor?"

"No, I've got Sara and Alistair looking into that this morning. But guess who's back in the country?"

Chef Maurice paused. Dorothy had been all atwitter about a member of the Royal Family who had cut short her trip to Australasia, raising speculation of yet another Royal Pregnancy, but something told him this was probably not who PC Lucy was referring to.

"Gaby Florence," continued PC Lucy. "Remember Miranda's ex-co-host? Apparently India didn't agree with her, so she flew back in yesterday. She lives in Hertfordshire, so I was going to drive over for a little chat."

Chef Maurice narrowed his eyes. "This invitation, it is *une ruse*, to keep us from the investigation of Monsieur le mayor. Hah, he has the police, how do you say, in his pyjamas!"

"In his pockets, chef," murmured Patrick.

"As you wish." PC Lucy shrugged. "I just figured you'd be interested in what she has to say. Plus this way, it saves petrol and all."

Chef Maurice gave this idea its due consideration. Getting a lift to Hertfordshire with PC Lucy did hold a certain appeal. His trusty little Citroën had been making some odd noises of late, and Arthur's idea of putting pedal to the metal was the liberal application of the footbrake whenever he came close to hitting the speed limit.

"Very well. Let us go to collect Arthur." He headed for the door, hesitated, then marched back to the table and dipped a finger in one of the virulent green blobs.

"Aha! As I thought. Avocado and garlic!"

With that, he stomped away, decanter and glass in hand.

While they idled outside Arthur's cottage, Chef Maurice gargling noisily with cognac, PC Lucy wondered if she was doing the right thing, bringing the two of them along on what was technically an official police visit. Chief Inspector Grant had already been none too pleased to have his team upstaged in the last two murder enquiries the year before, and expectations would be riding high on this current case.

However, when it came to interviews, she had to admit that Chef Maurice possessed the rare and little-appreciated skill of being an extremely charismatic listener. Perhaps it was something to do with his patent foreignness, but give him five minutes of sympathetic conversation, and he could make even the stiffest of British upper lips start to tremble.

Plus, the chef had been entirely correct in his suspicions that by bringing him and Arthur along, she was preventing them from spending the day rooting through Mayor Gifford's dustbins, climbing through his office windows, or even attempting a bout of breaking and entering in a hunt for more 'evidence'.

"Nice day for a road trip," said Arthur, climbing into the back seat. "We better get moving, though, before the neighbours tell Meryl I've been seen riding around in a police car again. So Gaby Florence is back from her stint of aura-cleansing?"

"So Adam Monroe tells me. She messaged him when she landed yesterday."

"Helpful sort of fellow, isn't he?"

"Troublemaker, more like. I get the feeling that sending us round to Gaby's is his way of getting back at her for having dragged him to the Spring Fayre in the first place. I hear a few of the tabloids got wind of them both being there, and have been raking up the mud again about him and Miranda. And Gaby too."

"What about her?"

PC Lucy swung the car out into the narrow lane leading out of Beakley. "Turns out there's more to her falling-out with Miranda than we thought. After she was dropped from the show, she apparently tried to run Miranda over with her car, just outside the TV studios. She missed her, though, and nothing concrete could be proved at the time. But she got a police caution."

"More than a bit of bad feeling there, then."

"Looks like it."

Gaby Florence lived in a cul-de-sac of low red-brick flats on the outskirts of Hemel Hempstead. From the lack of cars, it seemed that most of her neighbours were out at work. Even so, PC Lucy stopped the car several doors down from Gaby's—nothing got interviewees' backs up like parking a yellow-and-blue-checked car right outside their home for everyone to see.

"The cognac stays in the car," she told Chef Maurice, who looked puzzled at the idea that he would have brought his best cognac in to share with a complete stranger.

Gaby answered the door wearing a brightly patterned kaftan, black leggings, and jewelled sandals. Her long red hair was tied back with a length of beaded leather cord.

"PC Gavistone," said PC Lucy, holding up her badge. "We spoke earlier on the phone?"

"Sure, come on in." Gaby stepped back to let them through, with only the mildest of glances at Chef Maurice and Arthur. Perhaps she took them for plainclothes detectives or, worse still, thought PC Lucy, her superior officers.

"Can I get you something to drink?" said Gaby, in the tones of one completely disinclined to do so. "Except there's no milk in the house. I haven't had time to go out yet."

They declined, all three being fond of a little milk in their tea, and PC Lucy got down to business.

"Miss Florence, I understand you were at the Beakley Spring Fayre last Saturday, in the company of Mr Adam Monroe?"

181

Gaby's expression was sour. "Look, it was just a bit of a joke, okay? If I'd known what was going to happen, I'd have never gone along in a million years. I just thought it'd be a bit of a laugh, seeing Miranda's face when I turned up with Adam. I hadn't seen her in years, but I heard she never really got over him, even after all that drama."

PC Lucy thought about the framed photo she'd seen in Miranda's bedside table drawer.

"Did you speak to Miss Matthews at any point during the Fayre?"

Gaby hesitated, then nodded. "She came up to us, right at the start. All hugs and kisses and asking what I was up to nowadays, you know, just so she could tell us what *she* had going on. Some plans for a fancy country cookery school, she said. That made me laugh. That woman couldn't cook you a decent meal to, well, save her life. The only reason she was all right on TV was her culinary assistants doing it all for her. Why she would want to open a cookery school beats me. Guess she wanted to have everyone fawning over her in person."

"I see. And can I ask you where you were during the hours of half past twelve and quarter past one last Saturday?"

"So that's when it happened, then? Well, you can forget about me. I was with Adam the whole time, he'll tell you. We never left the Fayre."

"He tells me you disappeared for quite some time during lunch. While he was at the shooting stand?"

"Crossing all his T's, isn't he?" Gaby's lip curled. "Yeah,

I remember now, there was a giant queue for the loos. Feel free to check up on that one if you like. Someone must have noticed me, I was fairly hopping up and down for a pee."

"*Mademoiselle*, is it true that you once made attempts to run Mademoiselle Miranda over with your car?"

"I should have known that would come up eventually. Look, that was years ago now. I don't think I really even meant to hurt her. I was driving past the studio—this was a few days after they told me they were dropping me from the show—and she gave me this smirking kind of smile and waved, and I just *knew* it, right then, that she was the one responsible for the whole thing."

"Perhaps you will like to explain to us more, this 'whole thing'?" Chef Maurice reached into his jacket pocket and pulled out a somewhat squashed packet of teacakes, which he proceeded to hand around.

"The number of times I've told this story, and still no one listens . . . Okay, so Miranda and I had just signed up with this big production company to make a new cookery show. Bigger budget, better time slot, everyone was talking about this being our big break. So Gav, our manager, took us out to dinner to celebrate, and afterwards we went on to this club his friend owned, met up with some of his mates in the media. It was one of them who brought along the coke. I swear, I'd never thought to touch the stuff in a million years, but Miranda and Gav kept egging me on . . ." There was a hard, bitter look in Gaby's eyes.

"Anyway," she continued, "the pictures got out, and that was the end of things. Gav paid the press off, but the company wouldn't touch me with a barge pole after that. I thought it was just my bad luck, it could have been any of us in the photos, until that day when I saw Miranda standing there laughing at me, and it all fell into place. She was well into all her arty photography, lugging around that camera of hers, taking pictures of pigeons and tramps. And all of us, of course. The club wouldn't have let the press in. It had to have been her."

"So it was then you drove your car at Mademoiselle Miranda."

"I was just trying to scare her. I was horrifically sleep-deprived anyway at that point, what with all the drama. It was like going into a trance. Next thing I knew they were pulling me out of my seat and telling me I'd taken out a whole row of bollards. Miranda didn't even get a scratch. She made a big deal of it to the press, of course. And after all I did for us and our show! I wrote the recipes, wrote the scripts, taught her to look halfway competent on camera. Still, I guess she got what she deserved in the end."

"Not a kind thought, *mademoiselle*," said Chef Maurice, but handed her a teacake anyway.

"What made you return to the UK so soon?" asked PC Lucy. "I understood you had plans to be in India for the whole month."

"There's no law about changing your travel plans, is there? Yeah, I'd booked for the whole four weeks, but the place was a complete nightmare, nothing like the website. Great big ants all over the place, and they put me in this *hut* with a giant German woman who snored like a freight train. And then the woman who runs the whole show, she tried to steal my mobile phone! I mean, they told us we weren't supposed to have them with us, but it wasn't like I was going to call anyone, I just wanted it with me for emergencies. And for picking up my texts. Then they went and searched all our rooms. Well, that was the last straw! That and all that horrible vegetarian stuff they made us eat," said the co-author of the bestselling cookbook, *Cook It Right with Veg!*

Back in the car, PC Lucy let out a long breath. "Well, that was interesting."

"All rather too pat for my liking," said Arthur. "She was at the Fayre, has a damn good motive, and hightailed off to India right after the news broke. That doesn't say innocent bystander to me."

"It doesn't explain why she'd come back so soon, though. Even if the food was that dire."

Chef Maurice was staring out of the car window into Gaby's dark living room. "Perhaps we have it all the wrong way up," he murmured to himself.

"Have all what, old chap?"

"Remember how Madame Caruthers told us how Mademoiselle Miranda would steal the secrets of the other girls at the school? And remember Signor Gallo, with the story of Mademoiselle Miranda following him, to make plans of seduction in his direction?"

185

"Was she?" said PC Lucy, with some degree of horror. The Cowton Police Station put in the occasional late-night pizza order to The Spaghetti Tree, and the sight of Signor Gallo huffing and puffing his way up the High Street on his one-gear bicycle was not her idea of a particularly lust-inducing prospect.

"*Oui*, she followed him, but not to steal him from his wife. She wished, I think, to discover his secrets. To gather information to be used against him. Most probable, in the aim to stop his bid for the site of the cookery school."

"Blackmail?" said Arthur.

"Could be," said PC Lucy, as she turned the car back in the direction of Cowton. For some reason, she'd had trouble believing that the envelope Arthur had found in Mayor Gifford's study was evidence of a sordid affair. Blackmail, however, sounded much more up Miranda's alley.

"Change of tack, guys," she announced, a few hours later, as she strode into the main office at the Cowton Police Station. "We need to find out what Miranda Matthews was blackmailing Mayor Gifford about. And has anyone been to the shops? I'm dying for a cup of tea."

But PC Sara and PC Alistair were engrossed in whatever was showing on the latter's computer screen, and made no response.

"Hello? Earth to Sara? Al? What are you two up to?"

PC Sara managed to tear her gaze away from the screen. "Sorry? Did you say something about blackmail?"

"There's a chance Miranda was blackmailing the mayor about something. We need to find out what it was." She saw PC Sara's gaze migrating back to the computer even as she spoke. "What are you looking at that's so fascinating?"

"The lab sent us the encrypted files from Miranda's computer," said PC Alistair.

"And it looks like Miranda was up to quite a bit more than just birdwatching in her spare time." PC Sara swung the screen around to reveal a grainy photo of a couple, both in a state of some undress, taken through the slanted blinds of a tall window. Zooming out, their location was revealed as one of the second-floor rooms at the Cotswold Grand Hotel, an eighteenth-century building not far off the Cowton High Street. Tasteful wrought-iron lamps illuminated the handsome stone facade, and the full moon cast a soft glow across the cobbled street below. If you ignored the cavorting couple, barely visible at this distance behind the blinds, it would make a nice print for the living room wall, thought PC Lucy.

"The Carlton Arms is just across from the Cotswold Grand, and has a roof terrace which isn't used much, apart from in the summer," said PC Sara. "So we reckon Miranda must have set herself up there with a long-range lens." She clicked forward a few more photos. "These are just the beginning shots, by the way. It gets seriously kinky after that."

PC Alistair coughed, looking rather red around the collar.

"Now that's a back that could do with a good waxing," said Arthur, coming up behind them. "Is that who I think it is?"

"If you're thinking it's our illustrious mayor, then you're right," said PC Sara, clicking on through the photos.

Chef Maurice watched the increasingly scandalous photos flick by, tilting his head back and forth like a parrot watching tennis, as the couple managed a series of increasingly outré antics. "And the *femme*, is that not Mademoiselle Karole?"

"Right, I want all the evidence gone back over, in the light of all . . . this," said PC Lucy, trying not to stare at the large, now naked, male behind in the photo. "The Chief will want this case watertight before we make a move."

After all, she thought, it wasn't every day that you set out to arrest the Mayor of Cowton on the charge of murder.

CHAPTER 12

For the rest of the afternoon, the evidence flowed in fast and furious, like beer from a shaken barrel.

The heavy stump of piping found at the crime scene was identified as the same type of iron as the old Victorian stove sitting in the Giffords' back garden.

A pink bunny suit, original tail missing, was found hanging in the downstairs closet. The mud on the feet corresponded to that of the riverbank near Warren's Creek.

Scraps of photographic paper were recovered from the grate in the mayor's home study. (PC Lucy was surprised to find that, despite the room's cardboard books and reproduction artwork, it did contain a fully functioning fireplace.) Various hefty payments were also discovered going from Mayor Gifford's personal bank account to that of Miranda Matthews over the course of the last few weeks.

Faced with such accusations, Mayor Rory Gifford had decided to take a line of strenuous denial on all fronts. There had been no affair, he insisted. Yes, he had been at

189

the Cotswold Grand Hotel on March 8th, but only to attend a Rotary Club dinner. As to his connection with Miranda Matthews, he professed an even deeper level of perplexity. There had also been no blackmail, no payments, and certainly no plans to put an end to Miranda Matthews' scheme. A scheme he knew nothing about, of course. Because there had been no blackmail. Or affairs.

Yes, he had taken a walk down Warren's Creek that Saturday lunchtime. To admire the scenery, he claimed, and get away from the hubbub of the Fayre. He'd come across Miranda's floating body and immediately turned tail (presumably losing tail at the same time) and hurried back to the Fayre.

So why hadn't he informed the police straight away of his discovery?

Because he knew they'd take it the wrong way, just like they were doing now.

Mrs Angela Gifford, visited at her own home, confessed to no knowledge of her best friend's blackmail activities, nor of her husband's workplace philandering. He had, she admitted in tremulous tones, been guilty of a number of extramarital missteps during their first years as man and wife, but that had been a long time ago. Rory would never do such a thing now, especially not with a career at Westminster to think about. It had to all be some kind of misunderstanding.

As for Miss Karole Linton, it didn't take long for her to break down and admit to the affair, especially after being

190

shown a few of the more unflatteringly angled shots. She claimed to have been taken in by the mayor's silver-fox charms and his tales of woeful married life. However, she claimed she had no idea about Miranda's blackmail scheme, nor of Mayor Gifford's plans to put a rather terminal end to it.

All in all, by nine o'clock that evening, Mayor Rory Gifford had been taken into police custody on suspicion of the murder of Miss Miranda Matthews. Down at the Cowton Police Station, the case was declared as a large feather in the caps of all involved.

"Bah! It is all wrong. It cannot be!" Chef Maurice thumped his fist down on the table, sending pieces of cutlery flying.

Dinner service was over at Le Cochon Rouge, and the team was sat around the big table, Chef Maurice holding a spoon and a tub of the brown crab appetiser he claimed would not last until tomorrow, Dorothy inspecting the silverware for smudges, and Patrick applying ice to his shoulder to ease the strain caused by repetitive crêpe tossing after the night's dessert special of Crêpe Suzanne. (Similar to Crêpe Suzette, except with double the Grand Marnier and extra singed eyebrows.)

Alf had disappeared off somewhere, possibly to work on yet another apocryphal recipe.

"What do you mean, all wrong?" said Arthur, who had come round to deliver the news of Mayor Gifford's dramatic arrest. "They've traced the bank payments, and found Miranda's fingerprints all over that note we found in his desk. It's blackmail, all right. Fair and, well, unsquare."

"*Oui*, I do not say that Monsieur le mayor was not a victim of blackmail. But why then does he murder, when he already gives Mademoiselle Miranda what she asks for in return for her silence?"

"Maybe he couldn't trust that she'd keep schtum forever. Blackmail isn't an easy habit to give up, I hear. Can't see Gifford being happy, sitting in Parliament, knowing Miranda could come after him for more at any moment."

"And what of the pipe? To take it from his very own garden? It is an *imbécillité*!"

"I guess he thought it was safer than going out and buying a foot of iron piping. People might talk."

"And why choose the day of the Fayre?"

"Maybe something happened that week. Miranda wanted more from him, perhaps. He refused, and she was going to rumble him there and then. Big audience and all. A real bake-off bonanza."

"*Non, non.* This I do not believe. There is something here, something that we do not see."

"Come on now, old chap. You can't deny the facts. After all—"

"Bah, the facts! *Oui*, the facts give an answer, but it is not the correct one. I know it, in *here*." Chef Maurice prodded a thumb at his own ample stomach.

"It's terrible, seeing our politicians carry on like that," said Dorothy, holding a fork up to the light. Owing to

192

her bad knee, which had been giving her trouble these last few weeks, she'd spent the last half hour industriously spreading the news via telephonic means, and was now free to put her leg up and bask in the satisfaction of a task well done. "Young enough to be his daughter, that girl is! He should be ashamed of himself."

"I think he'll be a lot more than ashamed once the courts are done with him," said Arthur. "They're saying it's a life sentence, most likely."

"And to think he had the cheek to run for Parliament this next election! Say what you like, I was never going to give him my vote. Shifty kind of fellow, I always thought."

Arthur considered telling Dorothy that Beakley did not, in fact, form part of the Cowton constituency, but decided that such knowledge would simply rile the head waitress into further complaints about her rights to *not* vote for Mayor Gifford in the next elections.

"To tell the truth, I heard he didn't have much of a chance of getting into Parliament, anyway," said Arthur. "The current chap, Peter Ainsworth, is pretty popular with his constituents, and they're not the sort to fix something that isn't broken."

"Bah, this case, it is all broken," grumbled Chef Maurice.

"Oh, come on. You're just upset that for once it wasn't you who solved the crime. Justice has to come before ego, my friend. Just be glad they caught the chap."

"Humph. *Non*, I am certain that we still miss something. Something most important." He drained his mug of *chocolat chaud* and stood up. "I must go to think in the quiet. There can be no sleep until this case is solved!"

Ten minutes later, after a bout of sporadic thumping above them, the kitchen was serenaded by the snorting, chainsaw-buzzing sound of one slumbering chef, safe in the arms of Morpheus.

It was nearing midnight at The Skinny Jean, the latest bar favoured by the younger Cowton crowd. It had only opened a month ago, but already the dance floor had reached that critical point of stickiness whereby revellers were constrained to dancing on the spot, for fear of losing a shoe should they lift a tentative foot.

"Why the long face?" said PC Sara, nudging PC Lucy with her elbow and almost causing the latter to slip sideways off her barstool. "You've hardly said a word all evening."

PC Alistair, weaving slightly, appeared back at the table with a tray of drinks. "Two pints of Longhorn Bitters"—he placed one of the foaming glasses in front of PC Lucy—"and one, um, Goings-On on the Beach," he mumbled, handing the tall pink glass to PC Sara.

"Goings-On on the Beach is exactly what Miss Grumpy Boots here needs," she said. She clinked her glass against PC Alistair's pint. "We've just cracked a high-profile murder case, and unearthed a shocking scandal at the very top of local politics. So what's with all the moping I see here?"

"I'm not moping," muttered PC Lucy, who was slumped across the table, chin rested on folded arms. "I just think we might be missing something. If you listened to the way he was talking—"

"Oh, come on, don't tell me you fell for Rory Gifford's 'I'm so innocent, look at my chin dimple' routine," said PC Sara severely. "We got our man. So let's drink to us!"

She tipped back her glass, while PC Alistair sipped on his beer and looked surreptitiously down at the cocktail list. PC Lucy stared at her pint, sighed, then downed it all in one long gulp. The empty glass thumped back down onto the cardboard mat. "There. Happy?"

PC Sara regarded her friend. PC Lucy was a one-night-one-drink kind of woman. Downing her third pint in a row meant that something was definitely up. And she had an idea that it had nothing to do with death or politics.

"This is about that fellow of yours, isn't it?"

"'Snone of my business, what he chooses to do with his life."

"Rubbish. It's completely your business. Take a firm line and tell him he can't just go gallivanting up north and leave you here like this. Men appreciate a voice of authority. Isn't that right, Al?"

"Yes, miss!"

"That wouldn't work, not on Patrick," said PC Lucy, her head now resting back on the table. "He's not that kind of guy. His career means everything to him. He made a load of sacrifices to become a chef . . ."

"So you're happy to just let him up and go like that, then?"

"Course not." PC Lucy started to lift her head, then appeared to think better of it. "He's—" *hiccup* "—the best guy I've ever met. I thought this might actually—" *hiccup* "—*go* somewhere, you know? But they say, if you love someone, you've got to let them go . . ."

"Maybe I should leave—" started PC Alistair, looking uncomfortable.

"Oh, don't worry, Al. She won't remember any of this tomorrow."

"Course I swill," said PC Lucy, sitting up, indignant and slightly swaying. "Just like I'll remember the exact moment when the only guy I've ever really loved goes sweeping out the door—" She flung out one arm, almost taking out PC Alistair's half-finished beer.

"Oooo-kay, that's enough," said PC Sara, standing up and putting an arm around her friend's shoulder. "Miss One-Drink here needs to be getting home. You okay getting back, Al?"

PC Alistair nodded. As his two colleagues stumbled their way for the door, he took one final look at PC Sara's unfinished cocktail. Then he shook his head, squared his shoulders, and marched away without a backwards glance.

At the table directly behind the one recently occupied by three of the Cowton and Beakley Constabulary's finest, a dark figure, hat pulled down over face, watched them go.

196

A hand reached into a pocket, and there was a little click. Then the figure stood up quietly, and followed them outside . . .

CHAPTER 13

Hamilton the micro-pig woke the next morning to the sound of rustling outside his kennel, which was located in what had previously been Le Cochon Rouge's long-neglected vegetable garden. This overgrown field had been his home now for the last several months, and he was getting to be quite territorial about it.

His owner, the big fat man who gave him plentiful apples, had recently planted a small patch of carrots and crispy lettuce, and the local rabbit population had started dropping by daily to check on the patch's progress. Hamilton, who had firm ideas about where these carrots and lettuces should end up—namely, in his own feeding bowl—had therefore taken to patrolling the vegetable bed at regular intervals throughout the day. Micro-pig he might have been, but he was still comfortably larger than the average rabbit—a fact that both species had come to appreciate after a few minor tussles.

He stuck his snout outside, ready to head-butt any presumptuous carrot-curious rabbit, then gave a loud squeal.

The rabbits had decided it was payback time, and gone recruiting.

Traipsing about the field was a ginormous pastel-pink rabbit, attempting cartwheels, falling over a lot, and pausing periodically to wiggle its buttocks against the gnarled old apple tree over by the fence.

Every now and then, it would twist its head around to inspect its big white bobbletail. "Aha! I knew it!" was its war cry, before launching itself into another forward roll across the grass.

Hamilton retreated into his kennel to consider his options.

He had a feeling that his usual routine of grunting loudly and running full tilt at any bobble-tailed behind might not work in this particular case.

Then again, perhaps there would be no need. Unlike its smaller relatives, his newest furry visitor seemed hardly interested in the carrots and lettuces at all.

The kitchen crew of Le Cochon Rouge had all but forgotten their morning duties as they stood in a line at the edge of Hamilton's little field, watching the antics within.

Dorothy had rung up Arthur, on the basis that she'd never hear the end of it if he'd missed out on the current proceedings, and so he formed the end of their impromptu viewing gallery, taking the occasional sip from the tea thermos in his hand.

"How early did he start drinking?"

"I don't think he has been, luv," said Dorothy. "Came bouncing down the stairs first thing this morning and out into his car. Didn't even stop for a coffee. And then he came back all like this."

She waved an arm at the giant rotund rabbit still romping back and forth across the field, its pink fur rapidly turning to brown.

"If he thinks that pretending to go completely bonkers will make me choose to stay on here, he's barking up the wrong tree," muttered Patrick.

"Speaking of trees," said Arthur, "did you see him trying to climb the apple tree just now?"

"I think I shut my eyes at that point, luv."

They watched as the rabbit tugged once more at its tail, nodded with extreme satisfaction, then marched over in their direction.

"*Voilà!* I have gathered the necessary proof." It turned around and pointed jubilantly with both paws at its now mud-encrusted behind.

"I'm never going to be able to forget this image, am I?" said Arthur, mostly to himself.

"Proof of what, luv?" said Dorothy, handing a cup of strong black coffee over the fence.

"That he's lost every single one of his marbles?" said Patrick.

Chef Maurice reached around and tugged on the tail once more. "You see? It stays!"

"Please tell me you didn't nick that rabbit suit from the Cowton Police evidence closet," said Arthur.

"Eh? *Non*, this costume, it is my own. I made its purchase this morning at the Cowton Store of Fancy Dress. It is a little tight, perhaps"—he lifted two paws to the sky in demonstration—"but it has been sufficient for my experiment. *Regarde*, how firm the tail stays attached? It is impossible that Monsieur le mayor lost his own tail from a simple run through the woods. *Non*, his tail, it was not lost—it was stolen! Most likely cut away."

"Surely he'd have noticed someone coming at him with a pair of scissors," said Arthur.

"Ah, but remember what he said. That all day, the little children had come to pull at his tail. For someone then to come and cut it, without his notice, is not so difficult. In a big crowd, too, it could easily not be seen."

"So you're saying someone, the murderer presumably, cut off his tail and threw it into the woods, to put us off the real scent?"

"*Exactement!* I have thought much on this matter, and I am now certain that the true murderer will be caught. Today!"

"Cor. That's brilliant," said Alf, who was easily impressed.

"So who did it, then?" said Patrick.

"Ah, I cannot yet say. The situation, it is most delicate. And there are a small number of matters where I still make a guess. But, by the end of today, the answers will hide from me no more!"

He strode off towards the kitchens, but was headed off by Dorothy, waving a tea towel, who insisted he get out of

201

the grubby suit before he trekked a line of mud across the just-mopped floor.

A while later, Hamilton emerged from his kennel and, after a quick look around the field, trotted over to sit down in the middle of the carrot patch, where he remained for the rest of the day.

There was a small phalanx of journalists occupying the pavement outside Miss Karole Linton's terraced home, located down a narrow side road off one of Cowton's main shopping streets.

They snapped a few desultory shots of Chef Maurice and Arthur as the two of them pushed their way through to the front gate and let themselves in. Chef Maurice was carrying a wide cakebox and a folded note—the latter of which, after liberally applying himself to the doorbell with no result, he shoved through Karole's letter box.

"We also bring my most famous cherry clafoutis," he shouted into the opening, lifting the flap to allow the smell of buttery almonds and sweet cherries to waft on through.

"What was on that note?" whispered Arthur, trying not to make eye contact with the press mob, who had been out here since the early hours, surviving on cold tea and cigarettes, and were now eyeing the cakebox with the look of a herd about to charge.

The door cracked open, treating them to an inch-wide slice of Karole Linton's tear-streaked face. She looked them up and down, then swung back the door just enough to allow them to squeeze inside. (Given that one of her visitors was Chef Maurice, this required an opening of some considerable width.) Flashbulbs popped as the crowd of hungry journalists got in a few shots of Karole's bare hallway.

She slammed the door shut and leaned against it. She wore a baggy knitted jumper, jogging bottoms and fluffy slippers. Her hair was mussed and her eyes belied a night of tears and lack of sleep. In her hands, she clutched a dark green mug with the logo of the Lady Eleanor School for Girls.

Miss Caruthers' girls, thought Arthur, seemed to be making quite a name for themselves in the world. Though in Karole Linton's case, her recent appearance in the news would probably not be making it into the Spring Term newsletter.

"Do you really mean what you said in your note?" she demanded. "That you believe Rory didn't do it?"

"Well—" Arthur started, but was interrupted by a sudden elbow.

"*Oui*, that is correct. And you think the same, do you not, *mademoiselle?*"

She nodded fiercely as she led them through to her front room, dark from the tightly drawn drapes. Hot drinks were offered and politely declined. In Arthur's experience, upset women were generally incapable of making a good cup of tea.

"So tell us, *mademoiselle*, how is it that you believe in the innocence of Monsieur le mayor, after all the evidence that is presented?"

"I just knew it had to be a setup. Rory doesn't have a violent bone in his body. We visited a hospital once, and he practically passed out at the sight of a little bit of blood. He won't even kill the spiders in the office. I have to do it!"

"That's my job, too," said Arthur, who operated a swift and deadly arachnid-removal service in his own home. (In truth, Meryl was more than capable of dealing with their eight-legged intruders herself, but felt it her wifely duty to allow her husband to have the first turn, in the name of male ego maintenance. The same applied to jam-jar lids, the Sunday crossword puzzle, and any flat-pack furniture.)

"Did you know at the time that Mademoiselle Miranda was involved in the blackmail of Monsieur Rory?"

Karole shook her head. "I told Rory we should be more careful, that someone could have easily noticed us. We weren't exactly discreet, sometimes. He told me I worried too much, and anyway it wouldn't matter once . . ." She stopped, breaking down into a series of hiccuppy sobs.

"Once what, *mademoiselle*?"

"Once . . . we got married. He was going to leave his wife. He *was*, I swear," she said, glaring at them. "I know everyone thinks I'm an idiot, but it wasn't some tawdry affair like they all think. Rory's a good man. He just married the wrong woman, and didn't realise it until he met me."

Arthur nodded, recalling the various middle-aged men of his acquaintance who'd laboured for many years under the false notion of being in love with their wives, until a nubile young female showed them the error of their ways.

"And he had already told this to Madame Gifford?"

"I *told* him it'd be best to get it over with, before the campaign kicked off properly. He promised he'd tell her last week—but you saw them together at the Fayre, right? He clearly hadn't said a thing." Her fists clenched. "We had a big fight about that. He kept up this ridiculous pretence that he'd told her, that maybe she just hadn't understood. As if!"

"Ah, so you feared, then, that Monsieur Rory may have changed his mind?"

Karole looked down at the crumpled tissues in her fingers. "I don't know," she said in a small voice.

"Have you any idea why Monsieur Rory would have chosen to meet Mademoiselle Miranda at Warren's Creek? During the hours of the Fayre? It was a big risk to take, *non*, with so many people around?"

"Rory liked a bit of risk. But, no, I don't know why he had to meet her then. Maybe she'd asked for more money, and he wasn't going to pay up."

She shifted position on the sofa, causing a crackling sound from beneath the purple throw rug. She looked puzzled, thrust her hand under for a moment and came up with a box of expensive-looking chocolates, which she offered to Arthur and Chef Maurice.

"Scübadiva & Co.," said Arthur appreciatively, who knew his chocolates almost as well as Meryl did. "I remember the first time I visited their shop in Brussels. Nearly bankrupted myself on their eighty per cent Dark Blend."

"Pah, eighty per cent is too high," said Chef Maurice, who had a personal preference for a cocoa content of sixty-eight and a half. He selected a wild strawberry praline and held it up before him. "Monsieur Scübadiva, he is a craftsman of the highest level. You have excellent taste, *mademoiselle*."

"Oh, these came from Paul. You know, Paul Whittaker, Rory's deputy? He came over earlier, said he wanted to check I was okay. I guess everyone down at the Town Hall must have heard about it all by now, but he didn't say anything. Just told me to take my time, that there wasn't any rush to get back to work. I suppose given that Rory's down at the police station right now, that's no surprise." She blew her nose. "You know, I used to think Paul was . . . well, a bit sweet on me, but I guess the scales must have fallen from his eyes now . . ."

She gave a little laugh, with an edge of eighty per cent bitterness.

"So, what do we make of Little Miss Linton, then?" said Arthur, once they were safely ensconced back inside Chef Maurice's car, which still contained the lingering smell of cherry clafoutis. "Apart from her insistence that Rory Gifford isn't the murdering type, there's still not much in it to suggest he's not the guilty party. We know Miranda had the dirt on him, we know he had plans to meet her that Saturday. It's only his word against a bucketload of evidence. Not the most promising of scenarios, old chap."

"*Non, non*, do you not see? An idea, it begins to take shape. The camera that Mademoiselle Miranda carried with her, the pipe thrown in the bushes . . . A thought comes to me. Arthur, your diary. Pass it to me!"

"A man's diary is a rather private item," said Arthur, but handed it over nevertheless. It was an old-fashioned leather affair, complete with a section at the back containing a world map, a diagram of the London Underground, and a list of British sunrise and sunset hours—presumably so that if you found yourself deposited on some foreign shore, you would be able to a) navigate yourself home and b) do so by sundown.

Even so, it was fair to assume that Oscar Wilde, when speaking of the importance of something sensational to read in the train, had not been referring to the back section of Drayton's Pocket-Sized One-Week-To-View Double-Page-Spread in Dark Brown Leather.

It was, however, to this very section that Chef Maurice turned—in particular, the list of full and new moon dates for the current year.

"It's still a few days to full moon," said Arthur, peering over Chef Maurice's elbow. "So I'm afraid the werewolf attack theory is rather out, old chap. It was gibbous, if anything, on the day of the Fayre."

But Chef Maurice was not listening. He merely closed his eyes and nodded to himself. "*Oui*, if I am correct in my ideas," he muttered, "then it is certain that Monsieur Rory is an innocent man."

"In the eyes of the law, at least," said Arthur, still thinking about the grainy hotel photographs, which were proving disturbingly difficult to wipe from his mental library. "I don't suppose you've managed to dream up any evidence to prove your theory?"

Chef Maurice shook his head. "But, I have thoughts of a plan to prove the guilt of the true murderer, and so the innocence of Monsieur Rory. For this, we will require the help of many . . ."

Chapter 14

That afternoon, the newly formed Free Mayor Gifford campaign team met in the living room of the Giffords' Cowton residence.

Angie, of course, had been the first to sign up. "I never believed for a moment that Rory could have laid a finger on Miranda," she declared as she bustled around, plumping the cushions and straightening the tea coasters. "There's no crime in being in the wrong place at the wrong time. It was just lazy policing, if you ask me, the way they just turned up and took him away."

No mention of Karole Linton had been made thus far, and Angie's ready agreement to allow her home to host the campaign headquarters suggested, as Arthur had predicted on their drive over, that she was quietly prepared to stand by her man, come what may.

She had, however, looked less than convinced when Chef Maurice had declared his commitment not only to freeing her husband from behind bars, but also unmasking the true culprit in due course. Unperturbed, he put her lack of faith down to the fact she had never seen the Maurice Manchot Detective Squad in full action before.

It was now four in the afternoon, and two china teapots and an antique cake stand loaded with petit fours stood ready to welcome their visitors.

Miss Caruthers was the first to arrive. She embraced Angie, then turned to face Chef Maurice and Arthur.

"I don't approve of you raising the poor girl's hopes like this," she said, after Angie left to fetch another tray of scones. "She's got enough troubles as it is, without you giving her all these false expectations."

Nevertheless, she took up her seat at the end of the sofa. Soon the bell tinkled again, and Gaby Florence and Adam Monroe appeared at the living room door. Gaby's hair was arranged in wide, shiny curls and she wore a green-and-white cotton dress, while Adam Monroe looked like he'd just rolled out of bed and into the Fonz's wardrobe.

They settled themselves onto the chairs by the window, Adam's arm draped casually over Gaby's shoulder. Her India experience must have also prompted a sudden change of heart in Adam's direction.

"Why did you invite *them*?" whispered Angie to Chef Maurice, shooting Gaby a disapproving look. Clearly her loyalty to Miranda still ran deep.

"Mademoiselle Gaby and Monsieur Adam have both important knowledge of Mademoiselle Miranda's character. This is useful to us, in the discovery of the murderer. Remember, you agreed that the campaign must include all who may have knowledge to help us liberate Monsieur Rory. Oh, and I must mention," he added, "that in order that Mademoiselle Gaby would attend today, I told her you will consider her for a teaching role at your new cookery school." He moved away before Angie could muster up a reply.

Next to arrive was Karole Linton, pale but neatly turned out in grey trousers and a white blouse, accompanied by a solicitous but sombre Paul Whittaker. Karole sat down in the armchair furthest from Angie, who studiously ignored her presence, and struck up a hesitant conversation with Miss Caruthers about the headmistress's upcoming retirement plans. Paul Whittaker gave Angie's hand a brief squeeze, and assured her in low tones that everything was running smoothly down at the mayoral office, ready for Mayor Gifford's no-doubt imminent return.

"Are we waiting on someone else?" said Arthur, gesturing to the last empty chair.

"Our last guest will make a later appearance, I believe," said Chef Maurice, smoothing down his moustache. "For now, I think we make the start."

He turned to face the waiting group, who were sat in a semicircle around the coffee table, china teacups balanced on their knees.

"Thank you, *mesdames et messieurs*, for agreeing to come here today. We are all united, *oui*, in believing that Monsieur Rory Gifford, whatever his other crimes may be"—here everyone looked around at Karole Linton, who stared down into her tea—"is not responsible for the murder of Mademoiselle Miranda Matthews."

Miss Caruthers pursed her lips at this statement, but remained silent.

"And so, we must ask, if Monsieur Rory is not guilty of the crime, then who is?"

He paused here to take a dramatic sip of sugary tea.

"To discover this, we must make an examination of the personality of Mademoiselle Miranda. We learn from Madame Caruthers that Mademoiselle Miranda was in the habit of discovering the secrets of those she wished to influence. And from Mademoiselle Gaby, we know that there was little to stop her when she wished to get her way.

"It is a certain fact that Mademoiselle Miranda had many enemies. Yet, she always trusted that the secrets she discovered would keep her safe. She did not, I think, ever meet a person she could not control. Until, that is, she made her return here to the Cotswolds, and came again into the contact of a personality most *formidable*.

"Is that not right, Madame Caruthers?"

The room was still and silent as a bowl of setting jelly.

Miss Caruthers laid down her teacup with a gentle clatter. "Excuse me?"

"I believe that you take your retirement this year, is that correct?"

"It is, but I wasn't aware it had any bearing on our purpose here today."

"Ah, but this I will explain. It was at the Fayre, I remember, that you made a most interesting statement. That your sister, Madame Deirdre, began the making of pickles last year, in her own retirement. But you told us yourself, *madame*, on another occasion, that Madame Deirdre is the oldest of your sisters. Six years older, in fact. And yet you now look to retire, only a year later than your oldest sister? *Non*, this cannot be."

"I'm afraid that at what age I choose to retire from teaching is entirely my own affair, Mr Manchot."

"One may say so," agreed Chef Maurice, "but in this case, I believe your choice to have much significance to the discussion today. Because, I think, it was not just Monsieur le mayor who Miranda had looked to gain from in the last months. She came to you also, *n'est-ce pas*? A move that, how do you say, made a force of your hand?"

Miss Caruthers gave Chef Maurice a long look, then nodded. "Very well, I see you are quite set on dredging up the past. If that is so, I may as well be the one to put the facts on record. There is nothing in them that I am ashamed of. I take full responsibility for my actions.

"I had been in the employment of the Lady Eleanor School for some fifteen years when my sister Caroline, only a year older than me, was diagnosed with an acute form of leukaemia. In those days, successful treatments were few and far between, but I had heard news of an Austrian doctor who was producing some astounding results in his patients. However, his fees were not inexpensive, and our parents had left us little money on their passing.

"I was more than familiar with the financial situation at Lady Eleanor, having served as the temporary bursar for two terms when Miss Lovelace, may she rest in peace, was taken ill with a bad bout of influenza. The school funds were—and still are, I might add—in an extremely healthy state, and so I made my private case to Miss Lovelace. I might add here that she must have felt a degree of gratitude towards me, for having stepped in to keep her position open while she was in convalescence. My proposition was a simple one: I would borrow a sum of no little significance from the school accounts, to be paid back over several years at an above-average level of interest. It was not a loan a bank would have given to a man of my income, let alone an unmarried woman back in those times, and as such, I have no regrets in my actions. To see my sister celebrate her fiftieth birthday, something the doctors said at the time would be impossible, was worth any penalty I would have to pay in the future."

"But how does this involve Miranda Matthews?" asked Arthur.

"Ah, yes. Miranda. She was a pupil at Lady Eleanor during this time. In the Fifth Form, I believe. Miss Lovelace and I had believed our arrangement to be quite private to anyone apart from ourselves, but I imagine Miranda must have applied her skills of eavesdropping, and possibly lock-picking, to great effect during that period. Nonetheless, I had not the slightest idea that she had been privy to our discussions, until spring this year

214

when Miranda came to me, quite out of the blue, with a simply ludicrous request.

"She wanted fifty thousand pounds in fees to appear at the Beakley Spring Fayre, which I told her was completely out of the question, especially with the Fayre being an entirely charitable venture. She then, as you may now have guessed, threatened to expose my unofficial financial dealings to the School Board of Directors."

"And you let her tell them?" gasped Angie, staring at Miss Caruthers in horror. "I mean, she had no right. What did it matter what—"

"Calm yourself, Angela." Miss Caruthers patted her hand. "In the end, I went to the School Board and told them myself. I put it to them that they should of course demand that I go, and they agreed, but said it would be publicly announced as an early retirement, in light of my service over the years. I did not quarrel on this point. I suppose I have a little vanity left in me yet." She turned to Chef Maurice. "I trust that assuages your curiosity in the matter?"

"For now, *oui*, your explanation has been most suitable," said Chef Maurice, with a little bow.

Yet, thought Arthur, was it? An eminent career ruined by the greed of one ex-pupil. Could Miss Caruthers really be so disimpassioned about the loss of a position to which she had dedicated her whole life? From his memory, there floated up a vision of beads of water on a long tartan skirt . . . And something about children, playing down by the creek . . .

Chef Maurice appeared to glance at something outside the front window, then nodded. "But enough of the telling of stories to pass the time," he said, standing up in a flurry of cake crumbs. (Arthur saw Angie give a little wince.) "We come now to the reason that brings us here today. Because there are now not just one, but two victims in this crime. The first, of course, is Mademoiselle Miranda. And the second, if we do not succeed in our task, is Monsieur Rory Gifford, arrested for a crime that we all agree he did not commit."

"Well, when you say we all—" started Arthur, but he was quickly silenced by the combined death stares of Angie, Karole and Chef Maurice. "Never mind. On you go."

"So, we must ask the question, how did such a situation come to be? When we look at the clues, they point most strongly to Monsieur Rory. Too strongly, I say. The pipe from his own garden? The rabbit tail left for all to find? These, I think, were not a matter of coincidence."

"You think someone was framing him?" said Gaby, who seemed to be enjoying the current intrigue. Cowton was turning out more exciting than any ashram, and there was more cake too.

"*Oui.* Which leads us to the second question: was Monsieur Rory presented as a distraction, to simply throw the scent from the true criminal, or was there an aim more sinister? An aim to not just carry out murder, but, at the same time, destroy the career of a politician with much promise?"

"Surely not," said Angie staunchly. "Rory's a pillar of the community. Who could possibly want to do that to him?"

"Ah, a good question, *madame*. One, perhaps, that he can answer himself."

As if on cue, there was a knock on the living room door.

"*Un moment, s'il vous plaît.*" Chef Maurice scooted over to the door and flung it open with a flourish. "Ah, it is our final guest. Welcome home, *monsieur*."

The doorway was filled with the tall frame of Mayor Rory Gifford. PC Lucy hovered behind him, handcuffs swinging from her belt.

"So they've finally let me out," he announced, upbeat for a man who'd just spent the last night down in Cowton Police Station's clean but spartan cells. "Said some new evidence had come up, and I was free to go home. All due to Mr Manchot here. Boggled me good, he did, with his explanation, but I got it all by the end. Got brains coming out of his ears, this man."

Chef Maurice frowned, unsure if he liked this particular epithet.

"I knew you were innocent," cried Angie, launching herself into her husband's arms. "I knew it, I knew it."

"Well, this is all very well and good," said Adam Monroe, from his seat over by the window, "Mr Mayor here getting himself out of the clink, but I don't exactly see how this solves anything. Miranda's killer is still out there, right?"

217

"Not for long," said Chef Maurice, waggling a finger. "As I was saying before Monsieur Rory came to interrupt us, the solution to finding the murderer of Mademoiselle Miranda was to be found, not in searching her own life, but in the life of Monsieur Rory here. It was to become clear that the killer's real purpose was to bring down the life and career of Monsieur Rory."

"But who on earth would want to do something like that?" said Karole.

"Perhaps, *mademoiselle*, that is something that you may answer for us."

Karole's face blanched, as the room turned once more in her direction.

"I put in front of you, Mademoiselle Karole, that you knew all along that Monsieur Rory would never come to leave his wife. He made promises, *oui*, but in your heart I think you knew you were simply, how do you say, a thing of play."

"That's a lie," said Karole, her voice trembling. "Rory loves me, he'll tell you himself. He used to complain all the time about how things were at home, how *she*"—a manicured finger was jabbed in Angie's direction—"was always nagging him to get ahead at work, to make more money so she could have more things for the house. How he had to be bigger, more important, than everyone else. He couldn't wait to get a divorce and be with me instead. I loved him just as he was, not how I wanted him to be!"

Chef Maurice shook his head. "You, *mademoiselle*, knew already of how Mademoiselle Miranda was blackmailing him. Perhaps you even gave her the information of your places of meeting, so that she might follow you. Under the pressure of the blackmail, he would be forced to choose between his wife and mistress. So he did. Faced with a scandal, he made his choice. But in your eyes, he chose wrong. He ended the relationship. So you sought to destroy him, as only a woman who is crossed in love can."

"That never happened!" yelled Karole, all poise gone. "He chose me. Rory, tell them the truth!"

All eyes turned to Mayor Gifford who stood, with a giant-rabbit-in-the-headlights look, glancing back and forth between his wife and mistress.

"Come, *monsieur*, it is necessary that they know the truth."

Two great shoulders sagged. "I guess you're right. I should have done this a long time ago." He looked down at Angie, and took both her hands in his.

"Angie, my darling, I'm so very sorry for all the pain I've put you through these last few months. You've always been on my side, and I chose the most terrible way to repay you. But I need you to know something about Karole. Of course she has her faults, we all do. But I know that she, unlike you, would never stoop to murdering her best friend and framing her husband for murder.

"Angie, I want a divorce. And then I'm going to marry Karole."

There was a squeal and Karole bounded across the room and threw herself into Mayor Gifford's waiting arms. He enveloped her in a tight embrace, smoothing down her hair and kissing the top of her head. "It's all going to be okay now," he said. "It's all over, don't you worry."

"You haven't a clue about anything, do you, Rory?" Angie had taken a few steps back and now stood, shivering, her thin voice carrying across the silence like wind through a reed. "After all I've done for you, sacrificed for you, and you think you're going to throw it all away on a *tramp* like her? I won't let that happen!"

The cake knife, gripped tightly in her hand, was already making its way through the air when Chef Maurice launched himself across the coffee table and tackled her to the ground. The would-be weapon clattered across the floorboards, cake went flying, and PC Lucy stepped forwards to clasp a pair of handcuffs around Angie's flailing wrists.

The meeting was thus adjourned.

CHAPTER 15

The now-defunct Free Mayor Gifford campaign team, minus one founding member, had now decamped to the bar of Le Cochon Rouge, mainly because Chef Maurice was dying for a cup of coffee and no one (including the mayor) knew how to operate the machine in the Giffords' kitchen. So they had hopped in their cars and followed him to Beakley, not about to let him get away without a thorough debriefing on the heady turn of events just past. Mayor Gifford had decided to join them, if only to avoid having to sit by himself in an empty house with only a tray of pulverised scones for company.

"Come on, then," said Arthur impatiently, as they waited for Chef Maurice's coffee cup to fill. "When did you first twig that it was Angie Gifford all along?"

"Ah. This, I must admit, was a thought that happened much later in our investigations. When all the evidence showed the way to Monsieur Rory, yet still I was not convinced of his guilt, I began to think of what other solutions we may have missed. To frame a man for murder takes much planning. And who is in the best place to do this, if not his own wife or mistress?"

"So, it was just a guess, then?"

"A guess? *Mon ami*, you do not give me justice! *Non*, the first real clue to Madame Angie's true scheme was when I remembered the cake."

The little group around the bar looked at each other.

"What cake?" said Mr Whittaker finally. He was perched at the end of the row, hands on his knees, looking like a man who found the very idea of sitting on a barstool a tad risqué.

"The Smarties cake of many colours that Mademoiselle Miranda made in her demonstration at the Spring Fayre. Arthur, you remember?"

"I do, but I don't quite see—"

"Of course you do not see yet. I have not yet explained." Chef Maurice tutted, while the rich smell of freshly brewed coffee drifted over the bar. He took a deep sniff and sighed.

"Where was I? Ah, *oui*, the cake! And the photographs, we must not forget them. Remember the photographs taken of Monsieur Gifford and Mademoiselle Karole, through the windows of the Grand Hotel in Cowton?"

Arthur nodded, while the pair involved glanced down at their feet with looks of suitable chagrin.

"They were taken last month, in March, so the computer tells us. A very particular day, the day of the full moon, which showed most beautifully in the photographs.

"And then we think back to Mademoiselle Miranda's tale of inspiration for her many-coloured cake. She was in India in last month, she tells us, during Holi, the Festival of Colours. You see now? *Non*? The Festival of Holi is like the New Year of the Chinese—it changes each year, but follows the dates of the moon. And Holi is held on the *full moon* of the month, most usually in March. So, if on the day of the full moon, Mademoiselle Miranda was in India—as she showed us in the photographs of her holiday—how could she also be on the roof of the building which looks onto the Grand Hotel, taking photos from high above?

"*Non*, the blackmail photos, they therefore were not taken by Mademoiselle Miranda, but by someone else. Someone that would know her reputation for such schemes. It was then I thought of her best friend, Madame Angie Gifford."

"So it was Angie who was behind the whole blackmail scheme?" said Arthur.

"Look, how many times do I have to tell people, there *was* no blackmail going on," huffed Mayor Gifford. "I know I've made some mistakes this past year, but paying off a blackmailer? Unthinkable."

"What do you mean, there wasn't any blackmail?" said Gaby. "I heard the police found—"

"*Non, non*, Monsieur Rory speaks the truth. In fact, it was a part of the story that did not make sense, even from the beginning. That Mademoiselle Miranda would discover the affair of Monsieur Rory, but not tell her best friend? This was most strange. So I thought, what if there had been no blackmail to start with?

"Madame Angie, of all the people, knew well the character of Miranda Matthews. Perhaps Mademoiselle Miranda had told her of past schemes of hers. So it was not difficult to set things to frame her friend for blackmail."

"But why?" said Gaby.

"Ah, it was part of a scheme most intricate. A very dark scheme, born of revenge. You see, to divorce Monsieur Rory here"—he waved a hand at the mayor, who was sat with his soon-to-be new fiancée in his lap—"would not be sufficient punishment in the eyes of Madame Angie. She wanted his life completely made to pieces. And so she made a plan to frame him for the most terrible crime of all: murder.

"But there was a problem. Monsieur Rory, we saw, controlled all the finances. How would she survive when he was to go to jail? She had her teaching wages, but this was not much, and not enough for the creation of the cookery school she had dreamed of. But then, Mademoiselle Miranda, without so knowing, provided the final piece of her plan.

"In the contract they created for the cookery school, Mademoiselle Miranda would promise an amount of money for the project to cover the costs of the setting up of the school if she left—through choice or, in this case, through her death. It was at this moment that the sad fate of Mademoiselle Miranda was decided. Madame Angie would murder her best friend, and set up an appearance of blackmail to provide the motive required to frame her own husband for the act."

He paused to drop three large sugars into his coffee. "Does anyone here require *un café*?" he asked, waving the coffee tamper around. They all shook their heads, eager for the rest of the tale.

"Very well." He took a long sip. "So, it proceeds like this.

"Madame Angie pretended to have no head for technology, but this is not true, as we see from her kitchen. She had already made a discovery of the affair, from the reading of phone messages, and perhaps in watching the mayor and Mademoiselle Karole together. Now, with Mademoiselle Miranda gone to India, she uses her keys to enter the *appartement*, borrows a camera, and follows her husband to his meeting at the hotel. She then puts these photographs into the computer of Mademoiselle Miranda. She also leaves the envelope and a fake note from Miranda in the mayor's home study, ready for Arthur and I to find—it is not hard for her to use a paper that Miranda has already touched, so that her fingerprints show. She also burns the photographs in the fireplace, knowing it would eventually be searched. Last of all, she is the one who makes the payments from Monsieur Rory's bank account to Mademoiselle Miranda.

"And so, like this, the tale of blackmail is set, and it is time then for the second part of the plan."

"Bloody hell, there's a second part?" said Adam Monroe, his forehead already creased from the strain of thought.

"*Oui.* Madame Angie sets the date of the murder as the day of the Spring Fayre, an event where many people will be around, which will be of confusion to the police.

"Then, a trap is made for Monsieur Rory himself. Once more playing the idea of blackmail, she sends him a note pretending to be Miranda, instructing him to meet her at twelve forty-five at Warren's Creek. Miranda has, so Monsieur Rory thinks, photographs she wishes to discuss with him."

Karole looked at Rory. "So *that's* why you went down there that day? You thought she was going to blackmail you?"

"I had to see what she had to say, didn't I? I wasn't going to pay her off or anything."

Karole looked unimpressed.

"If I may continue," said Chef Maurice, "after Mademoiselle Miranda's cookery demonstration, Madame Angie goes to the dressing tent and urges her friend to follow her down to Warren's Creek, where the rare otters of the river have been seen. Mademoiselle Miranda, with no reason to distrust her friend, changes her shoes and follows her.

"At the creek, they stand on the jetty. Madame Angie, perhaps, points to the otters playing in the water, encourages Mademoiselle Miranda to take a photo. And so, with her victim now in distraction, she brings out from her handbag—remember, they are so heavy, these bags!—a

226

short iron pipe, held in a scarf or handkerchief. She is small but strong, Madame Angie. She strikes, hard, and Mademoiselle Miranda falls into the waters. The pipe, it is then thrown into the bushes, so that it may be found by the police.

"Then, at twelve forty-five, while Monsieur Rory comes to the meeting place, Madame Angie is already making her appearance back at the Fayre. Remember, *mon ami*, how she even comes to me and Patrick at the hog roast stand, and says she cannot find Mademoiselle Miranda and Monsieur Rory? Already, she wishes to plant the idea into our heads. And she plants more than just ideas. The tail we found in the bushes, that surely was put there by Madame Angie, not on the day of the Fayre, but when we went later to make a search."

He paused and scratched his head. "I think that is all. *Voilà*, you have the story. Complete."

There was a little smattering of applause.

"Amazing," breathed Karole. "I can't believe you managed to figure that all out yourself."

Chef Maurice puffed out his chest, apparently not the only male in the room who could be swayed by the charms of a young, wide-eyed *mademoiselle*.

"But what about that new evidence that turned up?" said Arthur. "The reason they let Rory go. Was that all just part of the ploy to get Angie to confess?"

"*Non*, the evidence, it is real. But perhaps 'new' is not the correct word. We had, in fact, already seen it. But we did not see!" He pulled out from one pocket a creased printout from the video of Angie pinning the new bunny tail onto Mayor Gifford's costume. "These new cameras, they are most powerful today. Mademoiselle Lucy and I watched the video again, but this time with more care. And then we saw!" He pointed at something glinting in Angie's hand. "Before Madame Angie makes the attachment of the new tail, she brings out the little scissors to cut the first tail off!"

Arthur remembered the little boy in the video. *Look, Mummy! She's stealing his bunny tail!*

"From the mouth of babes," he groaned.

"So Rory never actually lost his tail?" said Karole. "But I thought—"

"Ah, but when Madame Angie came to you and told you of the lost tail, she made sure that you were busy inside the face-paint tent and would not be able to see for yourself. And to her husband, she tells him she has a new tail to pin to him, and of course he believes her. Why should he not? Husbands, they let their wives brush the dust from their shoulders, the food from their beards. They do not stop to check in the mirror each of these statements."

"But what I still don't get," said Gaby, "is if she wanted revenge on him so badly, why didn't she just club *him* over the head instead?" She waved a hand at Mayor Gifford, who looked affronted at the suggestion.

"Ah, but that would not have been correct to her personality. Madame Angie, she told us herself, could never be a chef, because she wished to always see the results of her work. So for her, the best punishment for Monsieur Rory was a fate that he would have to live with. To be named a cheat and murderer for all to see."

"Revenge is a dish best served cold, eh?" said Arthur.

"*Oui*. But one, I think, that should be left from the menu altogether. It does not, in my mind, leave a very good taste at all."

CHAPTER 16

The thick padded envelope thumped down on the doormat.

Patrick looked up from his list of pros and cons. He'd spent the afternoon adding to the columns, in an attempt to drown out his thoughts about PC Lucy.

I'm sure it won't be a very hard decision, she'd said.

But had it been said with a tinge of sadness—or relief?

He'd be damned if he was going to move to the Lake District just to save his girlfriend the trouble of dumping him outright.

So he sat at the kitchen table of his little flat, carefully penning down new pros and cons, with the help of the Internet and an old copy of *The Intrepid Traveller's Guide to the North of England.*

Thump.

He stopped, halfway through the latest con on his list— 'The Lake District is home to two native British carnivorous plants'—and went to investigate this oddly timed arrival. It was getting dark outside, and far past the postman's usual hour.

He sliced open the packet, half-expecting to find some newfangled kitchen gadget, courtesy of a certain French chef. Instead, he found himself staring at a small handheld voice recorder.

Press play, instructed the message taped to the back.

So he did.

One minute later, the pros and cons list neatly filed in the recycling bin, Patrick was out of his front door and running down the lane, a huge grin on his face.

He had finally made his decision.

The little group of visitors had long since departed, and Chef Maurice and Arthur were sat at the bar, a celebratory bottle of vintage Port between them.

The front door banged open.

"You followed me around taping me?!" yelled PC Lucy, striding in waving a little black voice recorder. She was followed by Patrick, who was attempting to mirror his girlfriend's ire, and failing miserably.

"*Pardon?*" said Chef Maurice.

"Nothing to do with me," said Arthur.

Alf, who had been edging his way back to the kitchens, froze as four pairs of eyes zoned in on his back.

"It was all chef's idea," he mumbled, then made a dash for it.

PC Lucy turned her stare back to Chef Maurice, who was spreading a pungent lump of blue-veined roquefort onto a cracker.

"I thought it would be a good experiment to take a leaf from Mademoiselle Miranda's library," said the chef, unabashed.

"It was a private conversation! You had no right to send Alf tailing me around like that!"

"Ah, but it worked, *non*?" said Chef Maurice, with a glance at his sous-chef, who was grinning ear-to-ear.

"Looks like you'll be putting up with me a little while longer, chef," said Patrick, putting his arm around PC Lucy's shoulder. "And we've got news. We're moving in together."

"Congratulations," said Arthur.

"Ah, so you now decide to stay?" said Chef Maurice, with all the visible interest of one who has just been told the weather forecast in Sydney.

"With just a few conditions."

"Conditions?" Chef Maurice turned to Arthur. "Do you see what happens, *mon ami*? First, he threatens me to leave. And now, he holds me at ransom!"

"Well, let's at least hear these terms," said Arthur.

"First of all, I want to design at least three dishes on each new menu. *Not* including the vegetable side dishes," he added, as Chef Maurice opened his mouth.

"Humph. Very well. As long as we have no complaints from our customers."

"And secondly, we're reordering the ThermoMash." There was the sound of crashing pans in the kitchen. "We won't need it all of the time, of course, but it'll come in useful during busy shifts."

Chef Maurice appeared to consider this. "Of course, I will have to make a study of our accounts . . ."

"No problem," said Patrick, who had been budgeting for the last two years for such a purchase. "And last of all"—he gave a sideways look at his girlfriend—"you have to stop, and I'm just quoting here, understand, 'sticking your nose into police business'."

"Bah!" Chef Maurice waved a finger at PC Lucy. "I solve another case of murder, and see what thank you I receive? *Non*, that request, I refuse!"

Patrick gave PC Lucy a shrug.

"What do you think your mum's going to say about all this?" said Arthur.

"I already rang her up. She said she'd been expecting me to turn down the job, so she already had Jerome Archer—you know, head chef over at The Headley Arms in Warwickshire—lined up, just in case. I think she's secretly pleased. About us, I mean," Patrick added, squeezing PC Lucy's shoulder again. "Said I had my priorities straight."

"Pffft," muttered Chef Maurice.

"She also said to say hi to you, chef, and said it was high time we found you a 'nice lady to settle down with'."

There was a scrape of wood against stone as Chef Maurice almost fell off his stool. "Me? Never! If we learn one thing this week, it is that *les femmes*, they are much too dangerous!"

He stomped off to the kitchens, closely followed by PC Lucy, intent on a raid for more hidden recording equipment.

Patrick pulled himself up onto the stool next to Arthur.

"I'm thinking of taking Lucy away for a long weekend sometime soon," he said, with a quick glance towards the kitchen doorway. "Any ideas on where we should go?"

Arthur rubbed his chin. He'd been having thoughts in a similar vein, especially in light of recent events in the Gifford household. Wives, he decided, were definitely at their best when thoroughly appreciated.

"Well," he said, glancing up at the faded black-and-white photo over the bar, which showed the winding cobble streets of Montmartre at dusk, "Paris is always a good idea . . ."

J.A. Lang is a British mystery author. She lives in Oxford, England, with her husband, an excessive number of cookbooks, and a sourdough starter named Bob.

Want more Chef Maurice?

To receive email notification when the next Chef Maurice mystery is released, as well as news about future book releases by J.A. Lang, subscribe to the newsletter at:

www.jalang.net/newsletter

CPSIA information can be obtained at www.ICGtesting.com
Printed in the USA
LVOW07s1814260216

476854LV00008B/477/P